The Magic Trap

The Lemonade War Series: Books 1-5

The Lemonade War
The Lemonade Crime
The Bell Bandit
The Candy Smash
The Magic Trap

Praise for the Lemonade War Series

The Lemonade War
"Funny, fresh, and plausible." —*School Library Journal*

The Lemonade Crime
★ "Riveting." —*Booklist,* starred review

The Bell Bandit
"Davies portrays Evan and Jessie with subtlety and conviction. . . .
A fresh addition to a well-written series." —*Booklist*

The Candy Smash
"Another rewarding chapter book from the
Lemonade War series." —*Booklist*

The Magic Trap

by
Jacqueline
Davies

Houghton Mifflin Harcourt
Boston   New York

www.hmhco.com

The text of this book is set in Guardi.
The illustrations are pen and ink.

Library of Congress Cataloging-in-Publication Data
Davies, Jacqueline, 1962–
The magic trap / by Jacqueline Davies.
p. cm.—(The lemonade war series ; book 5)
Summary: "A magic show, card tricks, and a disappearing rabbit
named Professor Hoffmann—the Treski kids are at it again as
they try to put on a show in the face of an approaching
hurricane. But nothing prepares them for what blows into town
next: their long-lost dad" —Provided by publisher.
ISBN 978-0-544-05289-5
[1. Magic tricks—Fiction. 2. Brothers and sisters—Fiction.
3. Fathers—Fiction.] I. Title.
PZ7.D29392Mag 2014
[Fic]—dc23
2013024154

Manufactured in the United States of America
DOC 10 9 8 7 6 5 4 3 2

4500473398

For my father,
I. John Davies
(1932–1990).
Long gone, never gone.

Contents

Chapter 1
Illusion

illusion (n) something that seems to be one thing when it is really another; a magic trick

Jessie slipped her fingers along the inside of her closet doorjamb until she found the secret key. Silently, she unhooked it from the tiny nail pressed into the old wood and closed the key tightly in her fist. She liked the way the key became warm when she did this, the way it left a perfect imprint of itself in the soft flesh of her palm.

As quietly as a cat, she padded over to her bookcase, then paused. Was the Locked sign still showing on her door? Sometimes it flipped around if she closed her door too quickly. It would be a disaster if

THIS DOOR IS
LOCKED!

someone walked in while she was retrieving her lockbox from its hiding place. Even worse if someone walked in while the lockbox was open and saw what was inside. Jessie never showed *anyone* her saved-up money. That was just asking for trouble!

She opened her door and poked her head out to make sure that the Locked sign was in place. As long as the sign was on her door, no one was allowed to come into her room. That was the rule in the Treski house.

She could hear her mother packing in her room across the hall—a dresser drawer opening, the sound of footsteps crossing the wooden floor, hangers jangling in a closet. Jessie frowned. She didn't like her mother going away. But there was nothing she could do about it now. This was one of those situations where she would have to "adapt and evolve," as her mother sometimes said.

"Hey, Jess, can I ask you something?"

Jessie jumped at the sound of her brother's voice as he came up the stairs. Evan had been in the basement all morning, banging away on some old wooden boards. She'd thought she was safe from his prying eyes! She clutched the key more tightly in her hand.

"Not right now. I'm busy." Jessie started to retreat into her room, but she stopped when she noticed that her brother was carrying a book in his hands. Evan never carried books. He hated books. To him, they were the enemy, making him feel small and dumb. It didn't help that Jessie, who was thirteen months younger, was such a good reader. She looked at the book, wondering what it could possibly be.

It was old, whatever it was. The edges of the brown leather cover looked like they were crumbling, and the fancy gold lettering on the spine was half flaked off. Evan held it slightly open, his fingers curled around the edge to mark the page.

"It'll take two seconds," he said, half pleading, half ordering.

"Not now!" Jessie replied. She tapped the Locked sign on her door for emphasis, just so he'd remember the rule, and went back into her room, closing the door tightly behind her.

Still, she waited two whole minutes ("one Mississippi, two Mississippi, three Mississippi . . .") to make sure Evan had left the hallway and wasn't listening at her door, before she tiptoed to her bookcase and retrieved the lockbox she kept hidden behind the row of books on the top shelf.

The lockbox was heavy because of all the coins she'd been collecting for the past few months. It was surprising how many pennies, nickels, and dimes you could find if you just kept your eyes on the ground. Jessie's mom said that Jessie had a talent for finding money, but it wasn't a talent so much as a passion. Most kids wouldn't even bother to pick up a penny if they spotted it, but Jessie never let a coin pass without scooping it up and putting it in her pocket. She also saved her gift money and chore money, and now her lockbox was terrifically heavy and made the most wonderful rattling sound when she shook it.

Jessie sat cross-legged on her bed and opened the box. There were dollar bills and coins, the blue ribbon Evan and Jessie had won in the Labor Day contest last summer, several comment cards from her best friend, Megan, postcards from her dad, and a handwritten survey about love in the fourth grade, in which someone in her class had admitted to having a crush on Jessie. Anonymously! Jessie wasn't even sure why she kept that particular piece of paper, but every time she decided to throw it out, she ended up putting it back in the lockbox. It was evidence! Of what, she wasn't sure.

She stopped for a moment to look at the postcards from her dad. The stamps—from Turkey, Afghanistan, Congo, and Rwanda—were like little pieces of art.

Jessie liked the bright colors and strange pictures.

Her parents had been divorced for three years now. Her dad sent postcards and packages every few months, and sometimes he came for a visit. But it had been more than a year since she'd seen him. She thought about her dad every night before falling asleep, but she had learned not to ask her mother about him. She never got the answers she wanted.

Jessie organized the postcards from oldest to newest and put them aside in a neat pile. Then she turned her attention back to the lockbox. She wanted to take all the coins to the bank and exchange them for dollar bills. But to do that, she had to put all the pennies, nickels, and dimes into the special paper rolls that the bank gave her. Fifty pennies for the penny roll, forty nickels for the nickel roll, and fifty dimes for the dime roll.

Jessie knew exactly how much money she had in her lockbox: eighty-one dollars and forty-three cents. She kept a piece of paper with the current total tucked away at the bottom of the lockbox. Whenever she added more money, she changed the total.

INCOME/ EXPENSES	NOTES	CURRENT BALANCE
+2.00	chore money	$82.25
+0.25	found a quarter!	$82.50
−3.25	bought feather pen	$79.25
+0.01	found a penny	$79.26
+0.05	found a nickel	$79.31
+2.00	chore money	$81.31
+0.01	found a penny	$81.32
+0.01	found a penny	$81.33
+0.10	found a dime	$81.43

But eighty-one dollars and forty-three cents wasn't enough—not for what Jessie wanted. She wanted to open her very own bank account so that her money would be safe, no matter what. Once her money was in the bank, she wouldn't have to worry about losing it or someone stealing it or even the house burning down. It would always be there. Safe. *That's why they call it a safe!* She imagined the big bank vault where the money was kept. Because once your money is in a bank, it's *safe*.

Unfortunately for Jessie, the minimum deposit was one hundred dollars. She was a long way from that amount, with no prospects for earning money—big money—in sight.

"Jess, open up!" called Evan from the hallway.

"Locked!" shouted Jessie.

"Yeah, I know. So open up, would ya?"

Jessie closed the lockbox and shoved it under her pillow. Then she went to her door and opened it a crack.

Evan stood there with the old book open in his hands. His finger was marking a spot on the page.

"What is . . . ?" he said, pushing the book toward her. "I can't even . . ."

Jessie took the book out of her brother's hands as he walked into her room. Even though she was only nine, Jessie could read at a tenth grade level. She'd been tested. That's one of the reasons she had skipped a year, so that now Evan and Jessie were in the same fourth grade class.

She began to read out loud.

The Rabbit Box. This, as its name indicates, is a box for causing the disappearance of a rabbit. The opening is oval, measuring about eight inches by six, and closed by a double flap, divided down the middle (*see* Fig. 268). As the rabbit requires considerable space, and, moreover, involves the necessity of some sort of an inclosure to prevent an unexpected reappearance of the animal, it is a convenient plan to devote to it a small special table (*see* Fig. 269). The interior of the table should be well padded with hay that the animal may not be hurt by its sudden descent.

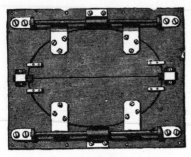

FIG. 268.

FIG. 269.

"What the heck is this book?" asked Jessie, flipping to the cover and staring at it. She read the scripty gold letters across the front: *Modern Magic: A Practical Treatise on the Art of Conjuring* by Professor Hoffmann. "Oh, this is one of Grandma's books! This one is *old.*" She turned to the title page.

"Published 1876!" she said. "Why are you reading one of Grandma's old books?" Grandma had more books than anyone Jessie had ever known, and now that she had moved in with the Treskis, her books were all over the house.

MODERN MAGIC.

A PRACTICAL TREATISE

ON

THE ART OF CONJURING

BY

PROFESSOR HOFFMANN.

With 318 Illustrations.

WITH AN APPENDIX CONTAINING EXPLANATIONS OF SOME OF THE BEST
KNOWN SPECIALTIES OF MESSRS. MASKELYNE AND COOKE.

Populus vult decipi: decipiatur.

AMERICAN EDITION.

PHILADELPHIA:
DAVID McKAY, PUBLISHER,
604-8 SOUTH WASHINGTON SQUARE.
PUBLISHED 1876.

"Because I need a big finish for my magic act," said Evan. "Everyone says you have to end your show with a big illusion. Not just some dumb card trick."

"Your card tricks are good!" said Jessie. Ever since Grandma had given Evan a magic kit for Christmas, he'd been practicing all kinds of tricks, which he called illusions. He could pull a quarter from someone's ear, make the ace of spades jump from the front of the deck to the back, and put together a piece of rope that had been cut in half. Sometimes he would tell Jessie how the trick was done, but usually he just said, "Magician's secret." Jessie knew he was trying to work up a magic act to perform for a real audience. She wished *she* could do something that people wanted to see.

"Not good enough," said Evan. "I need to make something *disappear.* That's what makes the great magicians great. David Copperfield made the Statue of Liberty disappear."

"He did not!"

"He did too. I saw it on Hulu. It was a trick, but no one knows for sure how he did it." Jessie watched as her brother pulled a quarter out of his pants pocket and started flipping it across the knuckles of his right hand. The coin looked like it was dancing across his fingers. These days, Evan always carried a quarter with him so he could practice anytime. With his other hand, he pointed at the open page of the book. "So, that rabbit box—it doesn't say how to make it?"

Jessie shook her head and handed the book back to Evan. "It's too complicated. And it's made out of metal."

"I know," said Evan, sitting down on her bed. "I was thinking maybe I could make it out of wood, though. I thought maybe Pete could help me. He's got a table saw and everything." Pete was the carpenter who had fixed Grandma's old house after she accidentally set it on fire. Pete could make anything.

"Pete's five hours away," said Jessie. "How's he going to help you build something?"

"I don't know," said Evan, staring at the diagrams. "I thought I could mail him a drawing, and he could cut the pieces, then mail them back to me . . ."

"Can't you just buy a rabbit box?" asked Jessie.

"Costs too much," said Evan. "Hundreds of dollars! I checked online."

Jessie knew Evan didn't have that kind of money. He probably didn't even have a dollar! "Professor Hoffmann doesn't do a very good job of explaining," she said. "Does he give instructions for anything else? What's that?" Jessie pointed to the book as Evan flipped the pages.

"That's the Sphinx. It's probably the most famous illusion of all time. You've got this little table with these skinny legs, and then the magician comes onstage and puts a box on top of the table, and when he opens the front of the box, there's a live head inside! And the head *talks* to the audience and answers questions. Then the magician closes the box, and when he opens it again, there's nothing but a pile of dust where the head was."

"How does he do that?" Jessie thought the floating head looked creepy, but if people would pay a lot of money to see it . . .

"Mirrors," said Evan, turning to the next page. "See?"

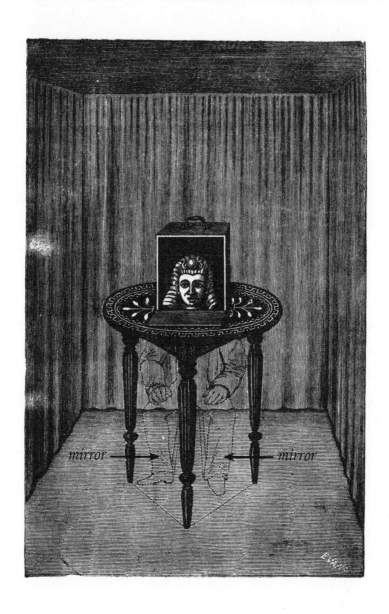

mirror ←→ mirror

15

Jessie looked at the illustration explaining the trick.

"The audience thinks they're looking straight through the legs of the table to the curtain in the back," said Evan. "But really they're looking at a reflection of the curtains in a mirror. So there's just a man hidden behind the mirrors with his head sticking up through the table."

"We could do that!" said Jessie. "We have a table with three legs. The one in the front hall."

"Mom's not going to let us cut a hole in her table," said Evan. "And besides, where would we get the mirrors? They have to be big."

"Not that big," said Jessie. She was starting to get excited. An idea was forming in her head. "The table is small, and the mirrors can be small, because I'm small—and I'll be the Sphinx!"

"You?" said Evan, scoffing. "Yeah, right. I'd like to see that. You talk too much!"

"You said the head talks to the audience!" said Jessie. She couldn't see why Evan didn't like her idea.

"Yeah, but it's—*mysterious* kind of talking. Not the way you talk."

"I can be mysterious," said Jessie. She would practice.

"Nah, Jess," said Evan, closing the book. "It just wouldn't work. You have to be really"—he stopped for a minute to think—"quick and quiet and . . . *smooth* to be a magician's assistant."

Jessie crossed her arms. It wasn't fair. She wanted to help.

"You know what you can do, though?" asked Evan. "Lend me twenty bucks."

Jessie stiffened. That was not the kind of help she wanted to give. "What do you need twenty bucks for?" Twenty dollars was a *lot* of money.

"Rabbits don't grow on trees," said Evan. "And they don't eat trees, either!"

"You're going to buy a rabbit?" Jessie nearly shouted.

"Sh-h-h-h," said Evan, pointing toward their mother's open bedroom door. "Cripes, Jessie! You see what I mean?"

"Mom is not going to let you buy a rabbit!" And suddenly Jessie remembered that she was mad at Evan. It was his fault their mom was leaving.

"Maybe I can talk her into it," he said. "It's worth a try. You can't make a rabbit disappear unless you have a rabbit to begin with. That's what Professor Hoffmann says."

"Yeah, well, Professor Hoffmann doesn't know Mom," said Jessie. She heard a car pull up outside and then a car door open and slam shut. Jessie thought this was weird, since Peggy wasn't supposed to arrive for another two hours. Peggy was Mom's best friend from when she was in elementary school, and she was the one who was going to stay with them for the week that Mom was gone. Abandoning them. *That's* what Mom was doing.

"But if she says yes, will you lend me twenty?"

"No!" said Jessie, moving to the window and peering down at the driveway. All she saw was a taxicab driving down the street.

"I'll pay interest!" said Evan.

Jessie's ears perked up. "How much?"

"I don't know," said Evan.

"Five percent!" said Jessie. "Per month!"

"Is that a lot?"

"Depends," said Jessie, shrugging. Five percent

per month *was* kind of a lot of interest. Especially since the bank these days was paying zero interest. But a bank wasn't going to lend twenty bucks to Evan.

The doorbell rang.

"Hey, Evan," shouted Mrs. Treski. "Can you answer the door?"

"Okay!" Evan called back, stuffing the quarter in his pocket. But then he turned to Jessie and said, "You do it. I have to find a rabbit box I can build."

"I don't want to answer the door!" said Jessie. "Mom asked you to do it." She thought of her lockbox, unprotected, hidden under her pillow.

"No rabbit box, no rabbit. No rabbit, no loan. No loan, no interest for *you*." He walked out of her room and into the hall, flipped the Locked sign on his bedroom door, and closed the door after him.

Jessie quickly hid the lockbox and the key in their hiding places and then hurried down the stairs, calling out, "Oh, fine!" over her shoulder. Five percent interest on twenty dollars would earn her a whole dollar. In just one month. Maybe she could lend money to other people, too. Maybe Megan would borrow from her. Maybe her friend Maxwell. Maybe even her mom would borrow from her. Money was always tight in the Treski house.

She got to the front door just as the doorbell rang a second time. If it was Peggy, Jessie was going to be stiff and a little unfriendly. She knew how to do this. She had practiced in her room yesterday. She would cross her arms and frown and march out of the room without even saying hello. Then Peggy would know and tell her mother how upset she was.

Jessie liked Peggy all right. She just didn't like it that her mom was going away.

It was the last week of May, but it already felt like the dead of summer. All in all, it had been a strange year, weather-wise. The winter had been so mild and spring had come so early that everyone said *this was the winter that never was.* Mrs. Treski had been shaking her head and worrying even more than usual about global warming. And now, at the end of May, the air was hot and humid. The windows in the front room were wide-open. As Jessie walked by, a breeze lifted the curtains and let them fall again, as if the window were sighing with pleasure. Jessie could hear a basketball bouncing in the distance and kids shouting. Maybe the person at the door was someone from the neighborhood coming over to ask Evan to play. Maybe it was the mailman with a special package for her.

The Treskis' front door always stuck in the summertime. Jessie gave it a good yank, but the door wouldn't budge. She grabbed the doorknob with both hands and pulled again with all her might. With a loud screech, the door flew open—and Jessie screamed when she saw who was standing on the front steps.

Chapter 2
Sleight of Hand

sleight of hand (n) a trick performed with the hands, requiring quickness and skill, such as making a coin appear or disappear; also called *legerdemain* or *prestidigitation*

Evan heard Jessie clomp downstairs to answer the door. If it was Peggy, he would just stay in his room. It wasn't that he didn't like Peggy; it's just that he felt as if he was getting a little old to have a babysitter. In three months he was going to be eleven. That was old enough to *be* a babysitter. In fact, sometimes Mrs. Nevya, who lived on their street, paid Evan to play with her two little boys while she did housework and made important phone calls. She knew Evan could be counted on to keep the boys safe.

23

Evan flipped to the section of the book that explained how to do sleight-of-hand tricks. There were seven basic techniques for sleight of hand, and Evan wanted to master them all: the palm, the ditch, the steal, the load, the simulation, the misdirection, and the switch. Today he was working on the palm. It was a technique that fooled the audience into thinking that your hand was empty when really you were holding something.

There were two ways to palm something: the finger palm and the classic palm. Evan examined the pictures carefully.

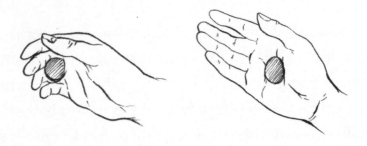

THE FINGER PALM   **THE CLASSIC PALM**

He could do the finger palm, no problem, but it was the classic palm that gave a better show. With the classic palm, you had to squeeze the muscles in your hand in just the right way—so that your palm held the coin or ball or whatever you were hiding—while making your hand look completely relaxed. It was hard.

Evan spit on his hands, then rubbed them together. He pulled out the quarter from his pocket and held it in his left palm. He waved his hand in a flourish. The quarter fell out and onto the floor. He picked it up and tried again. He didn't mind practicing. You had to practice if you wanted to be good.

Evan had always loved *watching* magic acts, but until his grandmother gave him a magic kit for Christmas, he had never thought about performing magic himself. As soon as he learned a few tricks—and discovered that he was pretty good, a *natural*—he'd been hooked. Every time he mastered one skill, he couldn't wait to jump to the next. Each skill was harder than the last, and pretty soon he was performing tricks that left Jessie and his mom asking, "How'd you *do* that?"

And magic was a lot like basketball. In basketball you had to move fast, you had to think fast, you had to drill over and over so that your muscles knew what to do before your brain even gave a command. And you had to know how to fake, to misdirect your opponent so that you could perform magic on the court. In Evan's mind, basketball and magic were almost the same thing. There was a feeling he got when he sank a shot, the way the ball left his fingertips, sailed through the air, then fell through the basket with barely a whisper. It made him feel as if everything was in its proper place, everything in the whole world was right where it belonged. Performing a magic trick—perfectly—made him feel the same way.

Evan heard the doorbell ring a second time and then the loud screech of the front door opening. Jessie shouted something, but Evan couldn't hear what. A minute later, his mom knocked on his door and came in.

"That must be Peggy," said Mrs. Treski. "I don't know what she's doing here so early. Maybe she thought there was going to be traffic on the drive. Can you help me close my suitcase?"

"Sure," said Evan, putting the quarter back in his pocket and following his mom.

"Wow," he said when he walked into her bedroom. "I didn't hear the bomb go off!" The drawers of her dresser were hanging open, and clothes were draped all over the bed, the chair, and even on the floor. There was a pile of books and magazines on her night table that looked as if it was ready to topple over, and at the foot of the bed was a small mountain of shoes.

"I had trouble deciding what to take. And I still can't close my suitcase." There was something in her voice that made Evan nervous. That made him put on his grown-up voice.

"Relax, Mom. It's not like you're going to the moon."

"Try to zip while I squeeze," she said, pushing down on the scratched purple suitcase. "It *feels* like I am. It feels like I'm going all the way to the moon."

One of Mrs. Treski's clients had asked her to attend an important conference in California so that she could write the promotional materials for a new product they were introducing. Evan didn't even know what the product was. Some kind of software. Mrs. Treski had lots of clients, and Evan couldn't keep them all straight. But this client was very big and very important.

At first she'd said no, explaining that she couldn't possibly leave her children for three whole days. "Family comes first," she had said to Evan and Jessie, which was pretty much her number one motto in life.

But the client had offered to pay her big money to do the job. And there were some serious repairs that needed to be made to their old house. So after a lot of thinking, she had finally agreed to go.

It was Evan who convinced his mom that she should stay an extra two days and have a little vacation. See the sites. Meet up with her old college roommate who lived in San Francisco. Have some fun.

"You never go anywhere, Mom," he had said to her. "You never have any fun."

She had looked at him strangely. "I have fun," she said. "I have fun all the time."

"Not grown-up fun," said Evan. "You just have fun with me and Jessie."

"I *like* you and Jessie," she said, laughing, but also

messing up his hair, as if she wanted this conversation to end.

"Parents need to go off by themselves sometimes," he had said, repeating something that Megan had said to him. Easy for her to say. Her parents were married, and they seemed to have plenty of money. At least more than the Treskis did.

Somehow he'd convinced her. If she had to fly all the way to California for business, she might as well stay an extra two days and have some fun.

But now that the suitcase wouldn't close, and the room looked like it had suffered an alien invasion, and there were reports of a tropical storm developing in the Caribbean that could move up the East Coast later in the week, making airplane travel difficult, Mrs. Treski was obviously having second thoughts.

"Maybe I should cancel this whole thing," she said, pressing all her weight onto the top of the suitcase. No matter how hard she pushed, Evan couldn't get the zipper to close.

"No!" he said, tugging with all his might on the stubborn zipper. "You can't cancel now. Peggy's here already and Grandma's with the Uptons and even Jessie has stopped squawking about it. You have to go. Just take something out," he said, pointing at the suitcase.

There was a loud clattering on the stairs, and then Jessie pounded into the room. "You have to see! You have to see! You have to see!" she screamed, grabbing her mother by the hand and pulling her toward the door.

"Jessie! Jessie! Slow down! What's going on?" Mrs. Treski allowed herself to be pulled out of the room. Evan paused, staring at the suitcase, wondering if he should open it and take something out while his mother wasn't looking. There was no telling what Jessie was so excited about. Sometimes it was something small that set her off. Maybe Peggy had brought a surprise with her. Maybe she had brought her cat, even though Jessie was allergic. Oh, brother! That would throw a monkey wrench in the whole plan. His mother was never going to make it out of the house.

Evan heard his mother say something, and then

there was a laugh. A man's laugh. A loud, booming, man's laugh. Evan felt a wave wash over him. It seemed to swell up through his stomach, drain all the saliva out of his mouth, and crash down to his toes.

He took a deep breath, pushed himself onto his feet, and headed down the stairs. By the time he reached the first floor and rounded the corner into the front hall, he knew what he would see. But he still couldn't believe his eyes.

Evan hadn't seen his father in over a year. The last time he'd come for a visit was a rainy, cold day in March, and he'd stayed for only half a day. He'd had a flight to catch. Evan couldn't remember where to. It was a country Evan had never heard of that had a lot of z's and k's in the name. Evan's dad was always flying somewhere, and he never carried more than a backpack with him. He liked to travel light. Over the years, Evan had come to think of that black backpack as just another part of his father's body. It was always there.

"Hey, Evan, my man!" his dad called to him.

Jessie was literally spinning like a top around him, shouting, "You're home! You're home!" Sometimes a wire tripped in Jessie, and she could go a little bananas. Evan's mom was trying to get Jessie to settle down by catching her shoulders so she would stop spinning. Evan looked at his mom and wondered if his parents had hugged when they first saw each other.

"Hi, Dad," he said, still standing on the stairs, eyeing the familiar backpack that leaned against the front door. Why was his dad here? Why today, when there were all the days that he hadn't shown up—birthdays and Christmases and whole summers. What made this the day?

"Come here!" his dad said, his voice friendly but a little too loud.

"Jessie! Quit it!" Evan commanded. Jessie was spinning so fast her arms were flying out from her sides like propeller blades on an old-fashioned plane. She spun too close to the wall and knocked over the wooden coatrack that stood in the corner. It crashed onto the floor, just missing hitting her on the head on the way down.

Evan's mother caught hold of her, but Jessie fought to wriggle out of her grasp. Evan hurried over to his little sister and grabbed her by the wrist.

"Come on, I have to show you something. It's important!"

"No! I want to stay with Daddy!" Jessie shouted, squirming away from Evan. But he was an expert at holding her by the shoulders in just the right way. It helped her slow down her breathing.

"We'll come back in a minute," said Evan firmly. "But I need to show you something first. Okay?" He steered Jessie toward the stairs, and she went along.

"We'll be right back, Dad!" she called over her shoulder. "Don't go anywhere! Don't, okay?"

Evan took Jessie into her bedroom and told her to sit down on the bed. Her cheeks were bright red and her face was sweaty. A strand of her hair was stuck to her chin.

"What do you have to show me?" she asked, her eye on the door.

"Wait here," he said. He disappeared into his room and came back holding a deck of cards. Then he arranged Jessie's desk chair and night table so that he was sitting in the chair with the night table between the two of them. Evan spread the cards on the table.

"A trick! That's not important!" she said.

Jessie got up to leave the room, but Evan said, "It's a good one. And I'll explain the secret at the end."

She hesitated, then sat back down.

"An ordinary deck of cards," he said, picking up the cards and fanning them out again so Jessie could see that the cards were in no particular order. "Now I'm going to tell you a story of four kings who were brothers." Evan quickly searched through the deck of cards and pulled out each of the kings.

Then he placed them face-down on his lap.

"Once again, notice that there's nothing unusual about this deck of cards." He fanned the deck out in his left hand and waved the cards in front of Jessie's face.

"Now the kings are going to travel to the four corners of the earth. The first king will go to the North." He slid the first king card, face-down, into the deck near the top. "The next will go to the South. The third will travel to the West, and the fourth will journey all the way to the Far East." As he spoke, he slipped the remaining three king cards into the deck.

"But the kings' troubles are just beginning. An

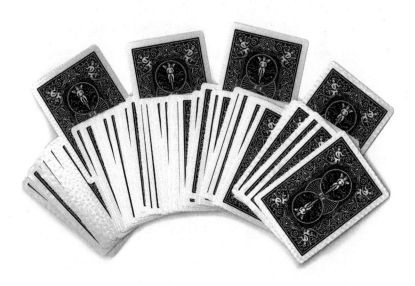

evil sorcerer has decided to create chaos by mixing Up with Down, In with Out, Right with Wrong! Watch as I shuffle the cards with half the deck face-up and half the deck face-down."

Evan turned half the deck face-up and shuffled the two halves together so that the cards were all mixed up: face-up and face-down. He shuffled again and again. "How will the kings ever find their way home? Can you help them? Can you find the four kings and bring them home?"

He looked at Jessie. Her breathing had slowed. Her eyes were on the deck of cards. Her hands were still at her sides.

He held the deck in front of her and said, "Put your hand on the cards, close your eyes, and say, 'Kings! Come home, come home, you will no longer roam!'"

Jessie was quiet, staring intently at the deck of cards. She placed her hand over them and whispered the magic words.

"Okay. See if you can find them." Evan spread out the cards on the night table, face-up. All of them were facing in the same direction. Except for four of them.

Breathlessly Jessie plucked each one of the four face-down cards and turned them over. There were the four kings.

"How did you *do* that?" she whispered.

"I didn't do it," said Evan, shrugging and gathering up the cards. "You're the one who made them come home."

"What's the trick?" she asked.

"The trick is . . ." said Evan, "that I got you to quiet down. You were going nuts down there, Jess." He started to shuffle the cards.

"But how did you . . . ?"

"I'll tell you later, I promise. But right now we have to go back downstairs. Can you keep calm or are you going to start spinning again?"

"But he's come home, Evan! He's finally home!"

"Yeah, I know. So?" Evan kept his eyes on the cards and made sure his voice was steady. "He'll be gone later today. Or tomorrow."

"No. Not this time," said Jessie, shaking her head. "He brought a *suitcase*."

Evan laughed, a short, sharp laugh. "He did not!"

"He did. I saw it. It's on the front steps, right outside the door."

"You're loco. Dad doesn't—"

"He *did*. Go look for yourself."

Evan stood up and stuffed the deck of cards in his back pocket, then headed for the stairs. At the top, he paused and said, "Jess, don't go nuts again, okay?"

"I won't," she said, and she grabbed hold of the back of his T-shirt, which was Jessie's way of holding hands because she didn't really like touching.

When they got to the kitchen, their mother and father were sitting at the kitchen table. Their father had a cup of coffee in front of him. Their mom was drinking a glass of water.

Evan's dad stood up to give him a hug. "Hey! Evan! Come here, man!"

"Everything okay?" asked Mrs. Treski, looking at Evan.

"Yeah, sure," he said. He walked over to his dad and they hugged, his dad lifting him off the ground. Evan wondered if his dad had hugged Jessie in this same way and if that was what had set her off. Why couldn't his dad remember stuff like that?

"I'm just going to check the mail," he said to his mom.

"It's kind of early, Evan," she said. "I don't think you'll find anything."

"Well, I'll look anyway."

Jessie had crept around the kitchen table and was now following Evan to the front door, holding on to his T-shirt again. Evan pulled hard on the front door. It was old and hung crooked on its hinges, so getting it to open and close was sometimes a project.

And there it was. Sitting on the front steps.

Just as Jessie had said. An enormous black duffle bag, stuffed full of enough clothes to last ... forever.

"See," she whispered. "He's finally come home."

Chapter 3
Cups and Balls

Cups and Balls (n) a classic magic trick that is more than two thousand years old, in which several small balls seem to appear and disappear under overturned cups; in his book, Professor Hoffmann called this trick "the groundwork of all legerdemain"

Jessie was sitting right next to her father when the phone rang. He had been telling them about something called an IED, which sounded to Jessie like a bomb because it had exploded in the road right in front of the transport vehicle he had been riding in. "If we'd been even twenty feet closer," he said, "we would have all been dead. I'm not kidding you."

"Jake!" Jessie's mom looked angry and tired at the same time. Mixed-up emotions. Hard for Jessie to read. "I don't want you telling the kids stories like that."

"Why not? They're old enough. They're not babies, right?" He turned to Jessie.

She nodded. "*I'm* not a baby." She glanced at Evan, who was slouching in the doorway. He was practicing with his quarter, making it dance across his knuckles, then disappear into the palm of his hand.

That's when the phone rang, so loud it made Jessie jump half an inch. Her mother hurried to answer it, as if she wanted to stop the horrible noise as quickly as possible. Jessie's head hurt, and her stomach felt achy, like it was pumped full of air and pressing out in all directions. She wondered if she felt this way because she was so glad her dad was home.

"Sometimes I forget what an American phone

sounds like," said her dad, leaning in toward Jessie. He flashed his special smile at her, his eyes crinkling up at the corners.

Jessie wished with all her heart she could say, *Me, too!* She wanted to be just like her dad. A prize-winning reporter. Brave. Fearless. A hero. Though she didn't really want to go to war. Too loud. Too messy. Too scary.

She looked closely at her dad. Taking inventory. That's what she called it. Looking to see what had changed since the last time she'd seen him. Everyone always said he was handsome, but Jessie didn't really know what that meant. Her whole life, she'd been hearing how handsome her dad was. One time she overheard her grandma saying to her mom, *Jake's biggest problem is that he's too handsome for his own good.* That confused Jessie. How could being handsome be a problem?

To Jessie, his face looked mostly the same: gray-blue eyes, straight nose, high cheekbones, and a strong jaw. He had thick dark hair that seemed just a little bit longer than the last time. There were also a few wisps of gray above his ears. That was new. Was her dad getting old? She knew he ran five miles a day, and old people didn't do that. Jessie looked at her father's hands, which were resting on the edge of the kitchen table. He had long fingers and strong hands. No ring. Jessie always looked for that when he came home.

"Hey!" said her mother into the phone. "Is something wrong? I was beginning to worry when I didn't hear from you." She walked into the dining room, which was now Grandma's bedroom, and closed the door behind her. Grandma was visiting her old neighbors, the Uptons, back in upstate New York. Jessie's mom had driven her there the day before. She was going to spend the week with her friends while Mom was away. It would have been too hard for Peggy to take care of Evan and Jessie *and* Grandma. Grandma had a way of forgetting things—like what year it was, or why she was living with the Treskis now, or even the names of her own grandkids. The Uptons, though, were used to Grandma and her forgetful ways. They were her oldest friends. She would be safe with them.

44

But now Jessie wondered if the phone call was *from* Grandma. Maybe there was a problem. Maybe she needed them. Maybe something had gone wrong. She tapped her foot against the rung of the chair to try to make the feeling in her stomach go away.

"Hey, Evan," said her dad. "Come over here."

Evan stuffed the quarter in his pocket, then slowly pushed away from the door frame he was leaning on and walked over to the kitchen table. His dad got up and stood beside him, pulling Evan in close and resting his hand flat on the top of Evan's head. "How much have you grown this year?"

Evan shrugged.

"Three inches and one-quarter!" said Jessie, jumping up and dancing around the two of them. "That's what Dr. Becker said at his last checkup. She said he was going to be as tall as you. Maybe taller!"

"Taller than me?" Their dad stretched up to his full height, straightening his back and puffing out his chest. "We'll see about that! I'm still growing, you know!"

"Are not! Are not!" shrieked Jessie, laughing and jumping higher in the air. She felt as if she had an electric current running right through her body. Her dad was so much fun!

"Jessie! Settle down!" said Evan, sounding just like their mom.

Jessie whirled around so she was facing her brother. "You're not the boss of me, Evan Treski."

"Fine," said Evan. "Let your head explode. See if I care." He headed for the stairs.

"Where are you going?" asked their dad.

"I've got things to do," said Evan.

"Like what?" Mr. Treski flashed his special smile.

"His magic act!" shouted Jessie, not wanting to be left out of the conversation. "He's going to put on a show, so he's practicing all the time."

"Magic?" said their dad, smiling even wider. "I used to know a few tricks. Well, one at least. I wonder if I remember it." He rubbed his hand along his cheek and scratched his chin. Jessie noticed that he had some whiskers growing on his face. She hoped he wasn't going to grow a beard. Jessie hated it when her dad had a beard. He didn't look like himself. "Will you show me a trick?"

Evan hesitated. Jessie couldn't understand why. Evan loved performing his tricks. And he was good! Why wouldn't he want to show their dad?

"Yes! He'll show you!" shouted Jessie. "Show him the one where you make the balls disappear under the cups. That's the best! Or the one with the water in the hat."

A minute later, Evan returned to the kitchen with three red plastic cups, which he set up on the kitchen table. Then he began the show.

No matter how many times she watched Evan do this trick, Jessie couldn't figure out how he made the balls appear and disappear under the cups. He would lift one cup: there'd be a ball underneath. Then he'd move the cups around on the table and lift the same cup—but there'd be nothing underneath. Then the ball would appear under another cup! And he did it all so fast. It was incredible. Evan had a book that showed the trick, but even so, Jessie couldn't follow it with her eyes.

"That was stupendous!" said their dad when Evan made three balls appear at the end of the trick. "You're *really* good!"

Evan smiled. It was the first time Jessie had seen him smile since their dad arrived.

"Can I try one?" asked their dad. "I don't know if I even remember . . ." He picked up the three balls and started juggling them. Jessie had never seen her dad juggle! "I'm just warming up," he said. "I'm rusty." He caught each ball, tossed it into the air, and caught it again in an endless loop that seemed to go faster and faster. All of a sudden there were only two balls! Where did the other ball go? It was as if it was there one minute and gone the next. Jessie kept her eyes fixed on the remaining two balls, which her dad was juggling even faster than before. Suddenly there was just one ball. Her dad was tossing it into the air and catching it in a looping circle.

"How did you do that?" shouted Jessie. Even Evan was paying close attention.

"Do what?" asked her dad.

"Make the balls disappear!"

"Did I make the balls disappear?" asked her dad. "Are you sure?" And just like that, there were two balls in the air again.

"Hey!" shouted Jessie. "There are . . ." But before she could finish her sentence, there were three balls dancing in the air again.

"One, two, three," their dad counted as he caught each ball, one at a time.

"Wow!" said Evan. "That was a really good trick."

Mr. Treski laughed and handed the balls back to Evan. "I haven't done that since college. I'm surprised I didn't drop all three of them."

"Can you teach me how to do that?"

"How good's your juggling?" asked their dad.

"Not . . . great," admitted Evan.

"Practice," said their dad. "A lot. Then I'll show you how it's done."

Jessie wondered if this meant her dad was going to stay for a while. Usually he visited for just one or two days. He always had someplace important he had to be. Even when he said he could stay longer, something always came up that called him away. But here he was making a promise. Maybe this time would be different.

Jessie's mom walked into the kitchen and placed the phone back in its base.

"What's wrong?" asked Evan.

Jessie looked at their mom. Her face looked like a weird mixture of too many emotions.

"Well!" their mom said, half laughing but also looking as if she might cry. "We don't have to worry about me not being able to close my suitcase— because I'm not going to San Francisco!"

Chapter 4
Switch

switch (v) to secretly exchange one object for another; (n) a sudden change in plans

"What do you mean?" asked Evan. His mother had been preparing for this trip for weeks. She'd done all the laundry in the house, put fresh sheets on the beds, and scrubbed the bathroom clean.

"That was Peggy on the phone," said their mom. "She's fine. She'll *be* fine. But she got in a small accident this morning, and, well, she's in the hospital with a broken arm."

"What bone did she break?" asked Jessie.

Evan glared at his sister. "She already *said,* Jessie. Her *arm.*" His brain was ticking through the possibilities of who could stay with them: Grandma, *no.*

Pria, their high school babysitter, *no*. Mrs. Blom, a neighbor who lived one street over, *no*.

"But *which* bone?" insisted Jessie. "There are three bones in the arm: the humerus, the radius, and the ulna." She tapped each part of her arm as she recited the three bones.

"I don't know," said their mother, shaking her head as if she still couldn't believe what she was saying. "All I know is that it's a bad break. They're pretty sure she's going to need surgery. And that means . . . I'm not going anywhere." She plopped down onto the seat of a kitchen chair. The chair groaned loudly, as if it might collapse in despair. "Goodbye San Francisco! Goodbye mini-vacation! Goodbye!" Mrs. Treski started to laugh, but Evan thought she looked as if she could cry at any moment. Each cheek had a bright red spot at its highest point.

"You seem relieved," said their dad, draining his coffee cup and then getting up for more. *As if he lives here!* thought Evan. *As if it's his house!* Although, in truth, it had been, once.

"Well, I'm not sorry to miss the airport and the

flight, that's for sure," said their mother. "But I was looking forward to seeing Joanna. And San Francisco. And then, too, there's the money . . ." Mrs. Treski was a freelancer. That meant she got paid only when she worked. There was no such thing as a steady paycheck in their house. If she didn't go on this trip, her client wouldn't give her any money. And that meant trouble when it was time to pay the bills.

"Oh, well," said their dad. "Freelance assignments come and go. You'll get something else, right?"

Evan wanted to shout, *It's not that easy!* What did his dad know about how hard his mom worked? Sometimes he sent money, but sometimes he didn't. His mom could never count on it. She tried not to let it show, but Evan had overheard enough phone conversations and seen the worry on her face to know that paying the bills each month was hard. Grownups thought kids didn't notice this stuff, but Evan did. And it stirred up in him that old fear that had set in after the divorce and never quite went away: that they would have to sell the house and move someplace else. Sure, it was a junky old house, with just about everything broken, but Evan didn't want to leave.

"Mom," he said. "You can still go. Jessie and I can sleep over at someone's house. Maybe Adam's or Jack's."

"I am not sleeping at someone's house!" said Jessie. "I can't sleep—" She looked at her mother, and Evan could see the panic in her eyes. Jessie had never slept at anyone's house except their own and Grandma's.

"Then someone can come here. There's got to be someone . . ."

"Evan, it's too late. My flight leaves in two hours. I can't just call someone up at the last minute and ask them to baby-sit for seven days. These things need to be planned in advance. I called Peggy about this trip two months ago."

Evan couldn't accept this. There had to be a way to fix it. "Mom, you have to go . . ."

She smiled and put her hand on his shoulder. He could see that she knew what he meant. It had always been like this. He and his mom. They just understood things about each other. "It's *charming* the way you can't wait to get rid of me, but—"

"Dad can stay with us," said Jessie loudly.

There was a moment of stunned silence. Evan looked at his father, then back at his mom.

"Oh, Jessie," said their mom, shaking her head.

"No!" said Evan. It came out louder than he intended. His father cocked his head and looked right at him, as if he'd been poked in the side with a very sharp stick.

"Your dad . . ." began Mrs. Treski, looking for words.

"Well, actually, Susan," said their father stiffly, "I could. After all, I am their dad."

Evan looked desperately at his mother, but she was staring at his father.

"Yay! Hooray! Hip hip hurray!" shouted Jessie, jumping awkwardly into the air and landing heavily on her feet. "This is great! This is the best!" She jumped up again and nearly crashed into the table when she came down.

"Jessie, stop," said their mother. "Dad can't stay with you while I'm gone." She turned to her ex-husband. "It's a whole week, Jake. You can't stay a whole week with the kids."

"Sure, I can," he said. "It's nothing. Seven days." He crossed his arms over his chest and leaned back in his chair, as if he were on the beach, watching a sunset.

"You never stay for seven days," Evan said harshly. "You never even stay for two."

"Well, this time"—he looked at Evan—"I'm needed."

"We don't need you," said Evan, the words sliding from his brain onto his tongue before he even realized he was saying them out loud.

"Evan," said his mother in her warning voice. "It's not a question of— Look, Jake. You must have somewhere else you need to go. You've always got . . . commitments. Your next assignment?"

"I'm between assignments," he said, shrugging. "I've got all the time in the world."

"The thing is . . ." Mrs. Treski looked down into the palms of her hands, as if she had the answer to a test question written there. "You can't . . . I mean, you couldn't just . . ." She looked out the sliding glass door to the falling-down porch and the over-grown yard beyond, then back at their dad. "If you say you're going to stay, you have to actually stay. You can't change your mind and leave. It's not like . . . They're kids. You have to stay."

"I *know* that." He seemed annoyed. Evan could remember the sound of their voices like this. His mother struggling to make her point. His father getting angry. He remembered these arguments. "But it's not like they're babies, Susan. You know, you always treat them like they have no common sense. Like they can't take care of themselves. In other parts of the world, they'd be old enough to herd goats or take care of a baby or run a house-hold. American kids . . ." He shook his head, be-cause they hadn't seen the things he had seen in other places. Evan could vaguely feel his father's disappointment in all of them. "You need to be tough in this world."

"I'm tough!" shouted Jessie. "Evan, too! Right, Evan?"

"Be quiet, Jess. You don't even know what they're talking about."

"I do! I do! Daddy's home. And he's going to stay with us. He said so!"

"The tribe has spoken!" said their dad, smiling and standing up. "Hey, come on, Su-su. We all know Jessie's the smartest one in the family, and *she* thinks it's a good idea."

Evan felt as if he'd gotten a swift kick in the head. It was always like this when his father came. Jessie spinning out of control, his mother sounding unsure of herself, nothing working out the way it was supposed to.

"Oh, for Pete's sake, Jake. Do you have to . . . ?" She waved in the general direction of Evan and Jessie, and Evan relaxed, thinking, *Of course she knows that she can't leave us with Dad. Everybody knows that.*

But in the end, she did. Dad repacked her suitcase so it would close, and she got into a taxi and drove away.

Chapter 5
Exaggeration

exaggeration (n) a technique in which a magician makes a showy, flashy gesture (also called a *flourish*) in order to misdirect the audience so they won't notice what the magician is really doing

"So what do you guys do for fun around here?" asked Mr. Treski, clapping his hands and rubbing them together as if he were getting ready to cook up a really great meal.

"Lots of stuff!" said Jessie.

"I'm going to my room," said Evan, heading for the stairs.

"What do you mean? I just got here. And now that Mom's gone . . ." He raised and lowered his eyebrows several times as if he were planning to do something Mom would not approve of. Something fun. Something exciting. Jessie felt her stomach flip then flop.

"What? Now that Mom's gone . . . you can leave?" asked Evan.

"Man, Evan," said their dad, shaking his head and smiling. "Give it a rest, would'ya?"

"I'm going to my room," Evan said again, and this time their dad didn't try to stop him.

"What's he so mad about?" muttered Mr. Treski as he walked across the kitchen and retrieved his backpack.

"Is he mad?" asked Jessie.

"Yeah, I would say so."

"But he didn't yell," said Jessie matter-of-factly.

"No . . ."

"And he didn't call names or say he was mad."

"That's true, but . . ."

"And his face was like this," said Jessie, making her face go completely blank, as if it were sand on a calm beach and a gentle wave had just smoothed it flat.

"Yeah, but Jessie, he was mad. Couldn't you tell?" Her father looked at her long and hard.

Jessie started to get that feeling of wanting to go up to her bedroom, close the door, and read *Charlotte's Web*.

Her dad pulled his phone from the side pocket of his backpack.

"That's a nice phone," said Jessie. It had a big color touchscreen, big enough that you could watch movies on it. Jessie's mom's phone didn't even have a screen. It was the kind that came free when you signed up for cell service, and it was at least five years old.

"Yeah," said her dad absently as his thumb flew over the screen, pushing buttons and looking at the text and images that flashed by. "I couldn't live without my phone."

"That isn't actually true," said Jessie. "That's *hyperbole*. We learned that word during our poetry unit with Mrs. Overton. Hyperbole is an extremely exaggerated statement that isn't true. So it's kind of like a lie, except that Mrs. Overton says it doesn't count as a lie, because it's a figure of speech. Which doesn't make sense to me. If it's not true, then it's not true. Like what you just said." Jessie didn't like exaggeration. She liked facts to be facts.

"Mmm, yeah," said her dad, never taking his eyes off the screen. "I get your point . . . but . . . just give me a second, okay? I've got to check the feeds."

"What are the feeds?" asked Jessie, perking up. This sounded like reporter talk.

"I'm hooked up to . . . well, they're like . . . they tell me what's going on in the world before anyone else knows about it."

"What's going on in the world?" asked Jessie.

"A lot. Every minute of every day. And I'm responsible for some of it."

"I thought you said you were between assignments."

"Yeah, well, a reporter is never really between assignments."

"But that means you lied—"

Jessie's dad held up a hand to silence her as he stared intently at the screen. Then he pushed one last button on his phone, and it made a chirping sound as he slid it into his back pocket. "But nothing's going on this second. At least nothing much. So what should we do?" He had a big smile on his face.

"I want to show you my room!" shouted Jessie.

They went upstairs, and Jessie showed her dad *everything*. The newest additions to her collection of trolls, all her homework and test papers for the whole school year, the books she currently had checked out from the library, and all the drawings and posters she'd made to decorate her room. Then she showed him all four editions of *The 4-O Forum*, which was the classroom newspaper that Jessie wrote and edited. He looked at each paper, but he didn't read any of the articles. So Jessie read the front-page story for each paper out loud to him so he wouldn't miss any of the good stuff.

"And I have eighty-one dollars and forty-three cents saved up," said Jessie proudly, folding up the newspaper. She thought of taking out her lockbox and showing him her savings, just so he would know she was really telling the truth, but then she remembered her rule about never showing her money to anyone.

"Good for you!" he said. "You're like your mom, saving money. Not like me!" He leaned back on her bed, casually resting against the headboard. Jessie's dad liked to lean on things. In fact, when Jessie's mom first met her dad, he was leaning against a cherry-red sports car. Not that the car was his, but *he sure looked good leaning against it,* her mom always said, laughing when she told the story.

"Can you please take your shoes off the bed?" she asked loudly, pointing at her father's feet, which were on top of her comforter and dangerously close to her stuffed animals.

Her dad swung his feet so that they hung over the edge of the bed. "Seriously, Jessie. That's a lot of dough for a nine-year-old."

"I'll be ten in four months."

"I know," said her dad.

"October eighth," she said.

"I know, Jessie."

"It's just that sometimes you don't remember," she said.

"I always remember," he said. "Sometimes I'm too busy to send something or call. You know, being a war correspondent is really tough, Jess. It's . . . well, you can't even imagine the things I see . . ." His voice trailed off, and for a moment he seemed to forget he was in the room with her. "But I always remember your birthday. And no matter where I am, I sing, 'Happy Birthday to you, Happy Birthday to you, Happy Birthday, dear Jessica Ann Winnie the Pooh Templeton Charlotte and Wilbur Too Treski . . . Happy Birthday to you!'"

Jessie laughed out loud when he got to the long, cramming-in-all-the-words part of the song. Daddy was the best at making up songs on the spot and telling jokes and being silly. She loved her dad! In fact, now that he was *here*, she was pretty certain that he was the greatest dad in the whole world.

Chapter 6
Rabbit Box

rabbit box (n) a specially built device that appears to be an ordinary box but actually has secret panels, mirrors, or compartments that can hide a rabbit within

Hey, Pete. How r u? I'm good. Ive got a faver to ask. Do you have scrap wood? I need to bild a box to make a rabit disapeer. Can I send u a drawng? And then u cut it and mail the peaces to me so I can put it togethr? Thx.
—Evan

Hey, Big Man! Good to hear from you. I've been wondering how things are with you and your family. All good? Sure I can cut the wood for you, but mailing it is going to be ++$$. Wood is heavy, dude. Do you have any scrap wood in your basement? Can you get someone to cut it for you there? There must be someone there who knows how to operate a saw. It's not brain surgery! At least not if you're careful! Ha ha! I saw your grandma yesterday. It's great to have her back in the North Country for a little bit. Come visit. All of you! I could use your help!

Stand tall, Big Man—

Pete

Evan stared at the screen, wishing he could re-write Pete's email. He wanted it to say: *Hey, Evan. Why don't I come down there and build the rabbit box with you? We'll do it together, just like we fixed your grandmother's house after the fire.*

Evan looked at the drawings in Professor Hoffmann's *Modern Magic.*

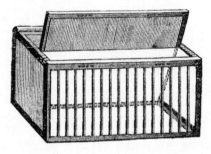

FIG. 308.   FIG. 309.

It looked so simple. It was just seven boards, two hinges, and a latch. How hard could that be? Except for the cutting. Pete had taught him how to glue, nail, sand, and paint wood. Working with Pete was like going to carpentry school, but more fun.

Evan looked at the pictures again, then picked up the book and headed downstairs.

Jessie and their father were on the porch in the backyard. Even though Memorial Day was just a week away and the weather was as warm as summer, the porch looked the way it did all winter—empty. The chairs and table were still up in the attic, and Mrs. Treski hadn't bought a single tomato, pepper, or basil plant. Usually by this time of year, the porch was overflowing with potted plants: calla lilies and marigolds, pansies and begonias, narcissuses and Cape roses. Every spring Mrs. Treski planted morning glories that would creep up and over the splintered and broken railing, twining their vines around the cracked wood. "It hides the rotted-out parts!" she would say.

But this spring had just been too busy. Evan

had never seen his mother work so hard. The porch looked as if it was stuck in winter.

Jessie was walking the perimeter of the porch, tapping each corner of the railing as she passed. Their dad was checking his cell phone, squinting at the colored screen in the bright afternoon light. Evan pushed open the sliding screen door and walked outside.

"Hey," said his dad, looking up for an instant. "The house is a dead zone."

Jessie laughed and started to repeat the words: "The house is a dead zone. The house is a dead zone."

Evan scowled. "Dad, do you know how to make things?" he asked. "With wood?"

"Wood? Yeah, sure. Well, no, not really. What are you talking about?"

"The rabbit box!" said Jessie, coming over to stand next to Evan and look at the page in the book he was holding. "For his magic show." Jessie stopped for a split second; then her face seemed to catch fire. "And I've got an idea! We'll sell tickets! I bet we could make fifty bucks, easy! That's big money! Enough to open my own bank account!"

"We're not selling tickets!" said Evan, suddenly embarrassed to even be talking about the show in front of his dad.

"Why not?" asked his dad. "Aren't you good enough?"

"He's great!" shouted Jessie. "But he needs a big finishing act. Something *kapow*. A blockbuster!"

"Where are you going to do it?" asked their dad. "An auditorium?"

"No," mumbled Evan. "I don't know. The basement, I guess." When he imagined the show in his head, he *was* in an auditorium, on a real stage, with hundreds of people watching. But he knew that could never be real.

"No way," said their dad, still looking at his cell phone. "Basements are for losers. You need something big. Impressive. You need a *stage*. Curtains. Lights. The whole thing. You need to look like a professional if you're going to charge money."

"We can build a stage," said Jessie. "A real stage!"

"Or maybe—" said their dad.

"But I'm *not* a professional," interrupted Evan.

"So fake it. That's what half the people in the world are doing. Act like a pro, people will treat you like a pro; next thing you know—hey, you're a pro." He folded his arms across his chest and leaned back casually against the railing.

Evan could have predicted what would happen next. Even Jessie shouted, "Dad, stop!" But it was too late. The rotted and splintered wood of the railing groaned and then gave way with a loud crack. Their dad just barely pulled himself upright before a chunk of the railing fell over the edge and onto the lawn, leaving a four-foot-wide gap.

"Whoa!" shouted Mr. Treski.

"You broke it!" said Jessie, clearly impressed.

"Well, better me than some kid, right? This whole porch is an accident waiting to happen. I can't believe your mother even lets you out here."

"It's not so bad," said Evan. "At least it wasn't until you ruined it." He watched as his dad wiggled the remaining boards of the railing, testing each one as if it were a tooth that needed to be pulled. "Leave it alone!" shouted Evan. "You're making it worse."

"This has to come down. It seriously isn't safe. And besides"—he swept one arm across his body as if he were introducing someone—"here's your stage."

"What?" asked Evan. Jessie looked puzzled.

"We'll take down the railing—which needs to come down anyway. Your mother's lucky she hasn't been sued yet. Then we'll set up chairs on the lawn and rig up a curtain. That should be pretty easy."

Suddenly Evan could see it. It would be perfect. A real stage.

Jessie was jumping up and down, hopping on one foot and then the other. "We'll do the show on Memorial Day. That'll give us a week to get ready. And I'll put out a special edition of *The 4-O Forum* with a front-page story telling everyone to come. And I'll make tickets to sell." She ran to the kitchen door. "We're going to be rich!" she shouted, then ran inside the house.

"Man, she sure gets excited," said Evan's dad,

shaking his head and smiling, as if he and Evan were sharing a private joke.

"She's not always like this, you know," said Evan. But how would their dad know? He hardly ever saw them, and when he did, Jessie was always wound up.

"So, what do you think?" asked his dad.

Evan knew what he thought. He thought his mom would not want them taking the railing off the porch. She would not want Jessie getting so excited that she couldn't stand still. She would not want to come home to find one hundred people in her back-yard.

But a stage. A real stage. And his dad was offering to help build it. They could do it together. Evan could feel his mother's disapproval, but he couldn't resist.

He held out the open page of the book to his father. "Can you build this?" he asked.

Chapter 7
Magician's Assistant

magician's assistant (n) the person who helps the magician perform onstage; the assistant is a highly skilled performer who often executes the most difficult maneuvers of an illusion

Usually Jessie loved school, especially on Mondays. She loved walking into the classroom first thing and finding the morning worksheet of math problems waiting for her on her desk. She loved talking to her teacher, Mrs. Overton, and hearing about what her cat, Langston, had done over the weekend. She loved reading and writing and science and social studies. Most of all, she loved taking quizzes, because she always got one hundred percent, and that was the best you could get. Jessie liked knowing she was the best at some things. It helped even out the other things she wasn't so good at.

But today she couldn't wait for the school day to end.

The day had gotten off to a bad start. Her father hadn't gotten up early enough to make breakfast for them. In fact, he hadn't gotten up at all by the time they headed out the door. It's not that Jessie needed anyone to make her breakfast. She knew how to pour herself a bowl of cereal. She was allowed to put toast in the toaster. But her dad had bought these special bagels from a deli several towns away, almost in the city, and she had wanted one, cut in half and toasted with cream cheese. But Jessie wasn't allowed to cut a bagel by herself. Even Evan wasn't allowed to use the heavy, serrated bread knife. If her mom had been home, she would have had the bagel ready for Jessie by the time she came downstairs dressed and with her hair combed. Then her mom would have helped her with her ponytail. Instead, she'd gone to school with several weird bumps in her hair.

Jessie also wanted the day to end because she wanted to get home and work on the latest edition of *The 4-O Forum*. She thought the front-page story about the magic show would drum up business for ticket sales. Plus there was going to be a special section on the weather, including an article on how to prepare for a storm emergency.

Jessie always included the month's weather statistics in *The 4-O Forum*. She loved collecting the data from the school weather station. At the beginning of the year, the fourth-graders used to fight

Weather Station Data

Day: __Monday__   Time: _8:52 a.m._

Thermometer: ___79°F___

Barometer: ___29.84 " ↑___

Weathervane: ___NW___

Anemometer: _20 - 25 m.p.h._

Rain gauge: ___0"___

about who got to climb out onto the flat roof of the gym and write down the data from the thermometer, barometer, weathervane, anemometer, and rain gauge that were mounted there. But now that the school year was almost over, she and David Kirkorian were the only two who still vied for the privilege.

Mrs. Overton had told them that the weather instruments were going to do some very strange things because of the tropical storm forming over the Bahamas and that they should all "keep a weather eye out." Already the air was hot and sticky, and there was no wind at all. It was as if the air had been sucked out of the atmosphere, and everything was heavy and still.

Mostly Jessie wanted the day to end because she wanted to ask Evan if he would let her be *in* the magic show. Yesterday she'd told him that she wanted to be his assistant, and he had said, "We'll see." So today she wanted to see.

"I'm home!" she shouted as she came in through the front door. Nobody answered. Usually her mom was in the kitchen, waiting for her to walk in the door. But of course, her mom wouldn't be there to-day. She was in San Francisco and wouldn't get back until Saturday at noon. Today was only Monday. That meant five more days.

Jessie checked the kitchen counter for a note. No note. Evan, she knew, was helping his friend Ryan carry home his social studies project: a Lego recreation of an Abenaki village in 1700. It took two people to carry the thing or all the wigwams would slide off the edge of the foam core.

Jessie turned on the kitchen computer, then pulled a black-cherry Jell-O cup out of the refrigerator. She'd had an idea in school that day about how she could convince Evan to let her be his magician's assistant for the show. She sat down at the computer and typed her question into Google: *How do I catch a rabbit?*

Jessie didn't really like animals. She didn't like the way they smelled, or that they peed and pooped unexpectedly, or the way they would sometimes growl or hiss even if you were trying to be nice. When she saw a dog walking down the street, she crossed to the other side. When she was at the house of someone who had a cat, she kept her arms crossed and her hands tucked under her armpits, safe and out of the way. And horses? Jessie wouldn't get within twenty feet of a horse. One kick and you'd be in the hospital with a broken cranium.

But Evan needed a rabbit, and Jessie wanted to be in his show. Maybe they could work something out.

The front door groaned open and Evan walked into the kitchen, slinging his backpack to the floor in the front hallway.

"Mom says *put it away*," said Jessie.

"Mom's not here," growled Evan.

"Still, you should," said Jessie. She wouldn't tattle on Evan; they almost never did that to each other. But Mom had promised to call every afternoon at four o'clock, and it was tempting. Then Jessie had a different idea. "I'll put it away for you!" she said.

Evan shrugged as if he didn't care, but Jessie could tell he was wondering what was up. She dragged his enormous backpack to the mudroom off the garage, where they kept their coats and shoes. They were allowed to dump their backpacks there.

When she came back into the kitchen, Evan was heading upstairs with a big bag of Doritos and the whole container of orange juice. When Jessie saw that, she had to bite her tongue to keep from reminding him that they weren't allowed to eat in their rooms. She followed him silently.

"So, can I be your magician's assistant?" she asked when they got to Evan's room.

"Mmm. I'll think about it," said Evan as he set up the small round folding table he'd brought up from the basement the day before. He was going to use it as his prop table—which is exactly what an assistant would be in charge of.

"You said that yesterday," said Jessie.

"Well, I'm saying it again today."

"But why can't I?"

"I didn't say you can't. I said I'd think about it."

"That's like saying no. That's what *grownups* do." Between Evan and Jessie, there was no worse insult.

Evan flipped the table upright, then pressed on it once to make sure the legs would hold. He looked right at her. "Here's the thing, Jess. You gotta be . . . I don't know . . . *smooth* to be an assistant. You have to be really quick and perfect and . . . you can't flub up. The whole show will be ruined if you make even one mistake."

"I won't! I won't! I promise you. I'll practice and practice. Just show me how and I'll do everything right." Jessie really wanted to be on the stage. She wanted everyone to see how good she was and applaud. And she wanted to trick everyone with the magic—knowing the answer to how something was done when everyone else didn't.

But mostly, she wanted to *do* something with Evan. They used to do all kinds of things together—have lemonade stands and build marble tracks and play games, like Stratego or Yahtzee or Clue. But nowadays he always had other things to do. It seemed as if he'd changed so much. Gotten older and more serious. More like the grownups. Jessie didn't like it.

"I don't know," said Evan. "This show is . . . important. It's not just a kid thing."

Jessie nodded her head. She knew it was important. First, because they could make a lot of money, and money was *important*—at least to Jessie. Second, their dad was going to see it, and she wanted to impress him so he'd know that she and Evan were really good at things. They weren't just babies. They were the kind of kids a dad would want to have.

"What if I get you a rabbit?" Jessie blurted out. "Then will you let me be your assistant?"

Evan gave her his smirky look, which meant he thought she was being a silly little kid and he was *so* much older. Jessie knew that look. Boy, did she know that look! "How're you gonna do that?" he asked, folding his arms across his chest.

"I've got it all figured out, Mister Blister. Don't you worry. But is it a deal?"

Evan waved one hand. "Yeah, sure. You get me a rabbit, and I'll let you be my assistant."

"Shake!" said Jessie, holding out her hand.

"Yeah, yeah," said Evan, quickly shaking her hand, then getting back to his prop table. "Good luck, little sister."

"I don't need luck," said Jessie. "I'm a *Treski,*" which is something her dad used to say to them when they were little, before he left.

*   *   *

The Google instructions looked easy. There was even a diagram.

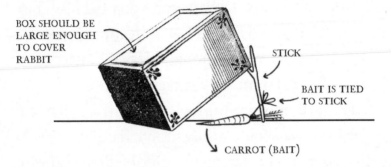

BOX SHOULD BE LARGE ENOUGH TO COVER RABBIT

STICK

BAIT IS TIED TO STICK

CARROT (BAIT)

She needed a box that was big enough to cover a rabbit and heavy enough that a rabbit couldn't knock it over. Then she needed a stick that was forked on one end so that the edge of the box could rest on it, and a piece of string that would pull the stick away when it was yanked. The last thing she needed was some kind of food for bait. A carrot seemed like the best option, but Jessie thought celery would do as well.

It all seemed pretty simple. One trap would do the trick, but since she needed a rabbit in a hurry, she decided to set five traps.

Luckily, the basement was filled with cardboard boxes of all shapes and sizes. Mrs. Treski was a bit of a nut about recycling. They used every box, bag, rubber band, ribbon, and scrap of wrapping paper over and over. Jessie had never even seen a brand-new envelope in the house. "Who needs them!" her mother would say. "They're killing the planet."

The problem with the cardboard boxes was that they were too light. But Jessie solved that problem easily. She taped rocks to the bottom of each box with duct tape. Jessie loved duct tape almost as much as she loved Post-it notes. She once made an entire backpack out of duct tape.

"What are you doing?" asked Megan, walking into the backyard as Jessie was positioning her five boxes. Megan lived down the street, and she was Jessie's best friend. Megan had lots of friends in school, but Jessie had just one.

"Be ve-w-y quiet. I'm hunting wabbit," said Jessie in her best Elmer Fudd voice. Elmer Fudd was always trying to catch Bugs Bunny, but he never did. Jessie hoped she would have better luck.

"Huh?" said Megan.

Jessie shook her head in disgust. "Don't you ever watch *Bugs Bunny*?" Even though Megan was her best friend, sometimes Jessie thought there was something wrong with her.

"How does it work?" asked Megan, ignoring Jessie's question.

"We need sticks. Sticks with forks in them." The two girls spread out, scouring the woods behind Jessie's house. There were hundreds of sticks, but it was hard to find ones that were the right size and were forked on one end. After about twenty minutes, they found five good sticks.

"What are you going to use for bait?" asked Megan as they tied a piece of string to each stick.

"Whatever we've got in the fridge." Jessie wasn't about to spend her money buying carrots when she figured a hungry rabbit would eat just about anything from the vegetable bin. In the end, they decided to use radishes because they were easy to tie with the string and because they looked pretty.

"Like little pink hearts!" said Megan.

Jessie frowned. "Rabbits can't see red." But she hoped they would smell the radishes and come hop-hop-hopping up to them. She *really* wanted a rabbit. Just one.

Jessie stood back and examined the cluster of rabbit traps. They looked a little rickety. She knelt down on the grass, bending over so that her cheek rested against the spiky grass and she could peer into the shady space under the box. It looked peaceful in there.

Megan lay down on her stomach and looked inside the box, too. "Do you think they mind being caught?" she asked.

"Rabbits don't think like that," said Jessie. "Their brains are the size of a walnut."

"But that doesn't mean they don't feel," said Megan. "Animals can feel scared or happy, even if they don't know why."

"I'll be nice to it," said Jessie. "I'll feed it every day and take it for walks. Or hops." Jessie giggled.

"But maybe it won't like that. Maybe it just wants to go hopping on its own and play with its friends."

"This rabbit is going to be a star on the stage. It'll be on the front page of the newspaper! People will clap for it." But even Jessie knew that a rabbit wouldn't care about that. Why did Megan always ask questions with answers that Jessie didn't like?

To change the subject, she said, "Put your hand down. On the grass. Like this. I want to test something."

Megan placed her hand under the box where Jessie told her to. Then Jessie karate-chopped the stick so that the box came crashing down.

"Ow!" shouted Megan, pulling her hand out from under the box.

"Did that hurt?" asked Jessie, her eyebrows wrinkling her forehead.

"Well, it didn't feel great!" said Megan.

"But it didn't hurt, right? I mean, your hand isn't *broken* or anything?"

Megan was rubbing her wrist where the sharp edge of the box had landed. "Why'd you do that?"

"I don't want to hurt the rabbit. By accident. Of course, the rabbit will be under the box, so it won't get whacked at all."

Jessie set up the stick and the box so that it was ready to go—but she had a prickly, uncomfortable feeling. To calm herself, she whispered, "Be ve-w-y quiet. I'm hunting wabbit."

Chapter 8
Gimmick

gimmick (n) a specially prepared object or device that makes an illusion work; one example is a rabbit box

Evan checked the clock on the wall in the basement: quarter to three. His mother had said she would call at four. They'd missed her phone call yesterday because of the difference in the time zones. But now they had the time difference figured out, and Evan wanted to hear her voice. He wanted to know for sure that she was "safe and sound," as she would say, and he wanted to tell her that they were putting on a magic show. But he didn't want to tell her what he was doing in the basement at that very moment, so he was hurrying to finish up.

89

Evan was sawing wood using the hacksaw that his mother kept on the tool shelf. It was not going well. He'd already snapped the thin blade on the coping saw—the scrap wood he was trying to cut was too thick for that—and now the bigger hacksaw was making a messy, jagged cut in the wood. Plus, his arm felt as if it was about to fall off, and he hadn't finished even one side of the rabbit box. He figured it would take him about three days just to cut the six pieces he needed. But he was going to stick with it. If you wanted to be a real magician, you had to know how to build your gimmicks.

In addition to listening for the phone, Evan had his ears open for the garage door. His dad was out, and Evan wanted to be sure to stop sawing and run upstairs as soon as his dad pulled into the garage. He could just imagine the lecture he would get about how he was too young to be using a saw and how dangerous tools could be and did he want to end up losing a finger? Or two?

Which is why Evan was particularly surprised when he heard his father's voice. "Hey, what's up?"

Evan jumped, the saw in his hand buckled, and

the piece of wood he'd been holding skittered forward and fell off the edge of the chopping block he'd been using as a tabletop.

"Hey, Dad," Evan said, as he retrieved the piece of wood and then casually put it aside. His heart was thudding in his chest. What kind of punishment would he get?

"Whatcha makin'?" asked his dad.

"Just that thing I showed you yesterday. That drawing. Of the rabbit box." Evan had made a careful scale drawing of the box and all the pieces of wood and hardware he would need to build it.

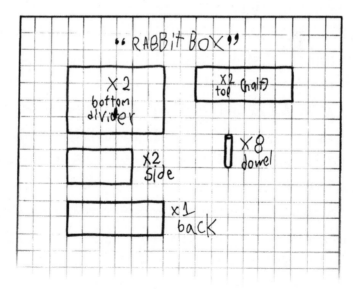

His dad hadn't seemed particularly interested yesterday, but today he said, "Hmm. I don't think you have the right tools to cut this kind of wood. It's too thick. You're going to end up with some pretty rough edges."

Evan couldn't believe his dad wasn't yelling at him for using the saw without adult supervision. In fact, he was acting as if it was the most normal thing in the world for Evan to be sawing wood by himself. Evan wished his mom could be that cool and not treat him like he was a baby all the time.

Evan looked at his dad. "Maybe you could cut it straight?" he asked.

His dad shook his head. "Nobody can cut wood that thick with this kind of a saw. You need a power tool to do the job. Which is why . . . I went to the lumberyard and had them cut the pieces for us."

Evan stared at his dad without saying a word. He couldn't figure out if this was a joke. "Are you kidding?" he finally asked.

"Nope. I made a photocopy of your drawing and took it to Diehl's. The guy there said you'd done a great job with your measurements. Very accurate.

He said he likes that in a builder. I told him, 'What do you expect? He's a Treski!'" Then he winked at Evan and headed for the car.

The pieces of wood were cut perfectly, each one square and neat. Just like Pete would have done. No sloppy edges. No mis-cuts. No splinters. Evan and his dad set to work joining them, first using wood glue and then carefully hammering in a row of finishing nails. Evan explained that you needed to spread the wood glue on both sides of the wood to be joined; it made a better bond. Pete had taught him that, and his dad seemed impressed.

"It needs to dry overnight before we can sand it," said Evan. "We'll use a coarse sandpaper to start, maybe ninety or a hundred grit, and then we'll finish up with a fine grit, like maybe one-eighty."

"You really know your stuff, Evan. Where'd you learn all this?" His dad was running his fingers over the hinges that they'd attached to the top of the box. The hinges were shiny brass—the expensive kind, Evan knew. He had measured and chiseled out spaces in the wood so that the hinges would sit flush. *It's the little things—the details—that make a project beautiful,* Pete had said to him last New Year's when they were repairing Grandma's farmhouse.

"I don't know. Guess I just sort of picked it up. You know, from people." Evan carefully put the hammer and chisel back on the tool shelf. He didn't want to talk about Pete with his dad.

The phone rang and Evan froze, staring at his dad. Then he raced for the stairs to try to get to the kitchen before the fourth ring, when the call would automatically be pushed to voice mail.

"I don't know why your mom still has a land line. No one has a land line anymore." His dad followed behind.

Evan didn't stop. "Well, *I* don't have a cell phone, and neither does Jessie." He felt kind of annoyed at his dad for not knowing this.

"That's ridiculous that you don't have a cell phone. I'm going to talk to your mother about that."

Evan reached the phone just before the fourth ring. As he grabbed it and punched the Talk button, he thought, *A cell phone! That would be so cool.* Some of his friends had them, and he'd been begging his

94

mom ever since Christmas. But she said he was too young.

"Hello?" Evan said.

"Hey! How are you? I miss you so much!" His mom sounded happy and a little out of breath.

"I'm fine! How about you? Was the plane ride okay?" He knew his mom had been a little worried about the plane ride. She didn't ride on planes much. Evan had never been on a plane in his life, so he didn't know what there was to be worried about.

"It was great, actually. Kind of fun. I had a nice person sitting next to me, and we talked the whole way."

A nice person? What did that mean? Evan decided he didn't want to know.

"How was school today?" asked his mother. "Did the butterflies hatch?"

"Not yet," said Evan. "But Mrs. Overton says it will probably be tomorrow."

"Good. You didn't miss it. I was worried they'd pop out over the weekend. Is Ryan back in school?"

"Yeah. But he went home early. He said he still didn't feel good."

"Poor guy! How about you? What have you been up to? I can't believe I haven't seen you in two whole days!"

"Nothing," said Evan.

"Nothing? Come on! You must have done *something* since I left."

Evan left the kitchen and walked upstairs. He definitely didn't want to tell his mom that he'd been sawing wood in the basement or that they'd knocked down the railing on the porch. But he also didn't want to tell her about building the rabbit box or even about the show. Why was that? And for some reason, he didn't want his dad hearing him talk to his mom. Usually it was the other way around—his mom was home when he talked on the phone with his dad. It felt weird having his mom be the one who was away.

Suddenly he didn't want to be on the phone at all. He wanted to work some more on the rabbit box with his dad.

"No, nothing. Just school. The usual stuff," said Evan. "Hey. I gotta go. I've got homework. Okay?"

"Wait! Hold on!" said his mom. Evan could tell

she was surprised. "Is everything okay there? Are you having fun with your dad?"

Evan hesitated. How much should he tell her? What if he said, *I'm having tons of fun with him. We spent all afternoon building together, and he showed me a juggling trick, and he's helping me build a stage for my magic show.* Would that make her happy or sad? Evan remembered how sad his mom had been right after their dad left. She had cried for weeks. Whenever Evan walked by the closed bathroom door, he could hear the water running and his mom sobbing. That had been awful. Jessie didn't remember. She was too young.

"Oh, you know. It's okay," said Evan.

"Really? I'm worried . . ."

"No, it's fine, Mom. Don't worry. Have fun in California. Eat a grape! Remember my state report in third grade? Grapes are California's number one crop. But I gotta go."

"Okay, okay. Busy, busy. Can I talk to Jessie?"

"She's at Megan's house."

"Oh. Okay. Well, I'll call again tomorrow."

"Great! Bye!"

As he hung up the phone, he thought he heard his mom say "Love you!" but he couldn't be sure.

Evan heard crashing on the stairs that could mean only one thing: Jessie.

She burst into his room. "Is that Mom? Can I talk?"

"You missed her," said Evan, holding up the phone and waving it to show that no one was there.

"I forgot!" wailed Jessie. "I was at Megan's, and then I suddenly remembered and ran all the way home. I want to call her back."

"Can't. She's at a conference, you know. She'll call again tomorrow."

"I don't want to wait until tomorrow." Jessie threw herself on Evan's bed.

Evan shrugged. He was old enough to know that sometimes you don't get what you want. Still, he felt bad for Jessie. He would have felt lousy, too, if he'd missed the phone call.

"Hey, did you get a rabbit yet?" asked Evan, smiling. Maybe he would let her assist him with one of the simpler card tricks, like Around the World. She couldn't mess that one up too badly.

"I don't know," said Jessie, jumping up from the bed. "I set five traps." She ran over to the window and stared out at the backyard.

"You set *traps*? What kind of traps?" Evan ran over to the window to look. He had a horrible picture in his head of those giant bear traps with the big iron teeth that could crush an animal's leg when they snapped shut. But when he looked out at the yard, all he saw were cardboard boxes tilting up like hats pushed way back on someone's head.

"Evan," whispered Jessie. "Look! One of them is closed up. I caught a rabbit!"

Chapter 9
Ditch

ditch (v) to abandon, get rid of, give up; in sleight of hand, to get rid of an object secretly

Jessie managed to get downstairs first, but just barely. Evan was right behind her, pushing and bumping in his effort to get to the rabbit trap before she did. They actually knocked the screen door off its track as they rushed onto the porch.

But when they finally made it to the traps, Jessie shouted, "Wait! Don't touch anything!" and they both stared at the boxes.

Two of them were knocked on their sides, the sticks fallen over and the radishes gone. Two of them were still set up with their bait intact. But one of them was collapsed closed, just the way it was supposed to when it caught a rabbit.

Jessie walked once all the way around the box.

"What are you waiting for?" asked Evan.

"We need a plan," said Jessie.

"What kind of plan? You pick up the box and grab the rabbit."

"It's not that simple," said Jessie. "What if the rabbit bites?"

"Rabbits don't bite!"

"They might. They have teeth. Two sets of incisors. When they get scared, they sometimes lunge." And suddenly Jessie thought of the rabbit being scared, which hadn't occurred to her before. And she thought about being inside that small, closed, dark space, and her skin got shivery. Jessie didn't like to be closed up in dark spaces.

"*I'm* not scared," said Evan. "It's just a rabbit. You pick up the box and I'll grab it."

"You need gloves," said Jessie. "Something that will protect you in case it scratches."

"Rabbits don't scratch."

"They have claws."

"How do you know so much about rabbits?"

"I read," said Jessie. Which was true. She had spent an hour on Sunday night reading about rabbits. And although she hadn't come across a single story of a rabbit attacking a human being, rabbits had all the necessary body parts: sharp teeth, claws, and powerful kicking legs. You couldn't be too careful. That was Jessie's motto. "Get the oven mitts from the kitchen. They'll protect your hands and arms."

A minute later Evan came out with the bright red quilted mitts on his hands. He looked like a gingerbread man. "I'm never going to be able to catch the rabbit wearing these."

"You don't have to catch it. Just keep it from running away. I'll flip the box over and scoop up the rabbit, like a bulldozer. Then you cover the top of the box with your hands. Okay?"

"Okay." He crouched down so that he was right in front of the box, like a baseball catcher in front of home plate.

"But Evan, you have to be really careful. Don't grab it, because rabbits have special bones that can break like that." Jessie snapped her fingers to show him how delicate a rabbit's skeleton is. "It's what helps them squeeze into tiny hiding places."

Evan stood up. "Maybe we shouldn't do this, Jess. What if the rabbit's already hurt under there?" Jessie could see the worried look on Evan's face. That was an easy look to spot. His eyebrows came down on the insides and he made this squiggly-line smile that wasn't happy or sad. It was worried.

But there was no *evidence* that the rabbit was hurt, so Jessie wasn't going to let herself get all worried for no reason. The only thing that made sense was to lift the box and find out. That's what a scientist would do, and Jessie liked science. Much more than animals.

"We have to look," she said sternly. "Are you ready?"

Evan crouched down. "Ready."

"One, two, three, *lift!*" Jessie flipped the box over onto its side and scooped it at the same time that Evan rushed forward, his oven mitts acting as a barricade. Something dark was moving on the grass;

then there was a scratching and scrabbling sound in the box, and Jessie finished scooping the box so that it sat on the grass with its opening facing up to the sky.

"Wow, we got it!" shouted Evan, and they both peered into the box.

There at the bottom was a small dark brown animal, frantically running along the edge of the box.

It was not a rabbit.

"What is that?" asked Evan.

"It's a mole," said Jessie, feeling as if she'd just been given a birthday present and opened it up, only to find out it was socks.

"A mole?" said Evan. "I didn't know we had moles in the yard."

Jessie looked at Evan. Her plan was ruined. They didn't have a rabbit, and now Evan wouldn't let her be his assistant. She would be stuck selling tickets and ushering people to their seats. "I don't suppose you could use a mole in your magic act?"

"Nah," said Evan. "That little guy would just tunnel his way out. Look at him go!" It was true.

The mole was already scraping at the side of the box with his two large paws. "But Jess, I don't think you should try to catch any more rabbits. You know?"

Jessie nodded. If the rabbit had been hurt—even if the mole had been hurt!—she would have felt terrible. She didn't like animals, but she didn't want to hurt them. Last winter she'd even stood up to a couple of boys who were doing mean things to a frog. And the boys had been older! But Jessie had stood her ground and made them stop. Almost single-handedly. She tilted the box and watched the mole disappear into the woods.

"But now you don't have a rabbit for your show," she said.

"It's okay. I'll use Peter Rabbit." Evan had an old stuffed Peter Rabbit toy, complete with a blue jacket and an orange carrot.

"It's not as good," said Jessie, shaking her head. Real magicians didn't use toys. "A live rabbit would be better."

"Yeah, but what are you gonna do? It'll be *okay* with the toy. I'll still make it appear." Evan picked up the sticks and threw them far into the woods. Jessie started stacking the boxes. With all the rocks taped on, they were really heavy.

"Hey, Jess," said Evan. "You were pretty smooth with flipping the box and catching the mole. You were fast, and you did it just right. I don't think I could have done as good."

Jessie smiled. "I kept my head! I didn't panic."

"No, you didn't." Evan looked off into the woods for a minute. "So you want to be my assistant?"

"Really? Can I?" Jessie jumped up and down. "Yes! I'll be so good, I promise! I'll practice and practice and be super smooth."

"Well, we should start *now*. The show's in a week. That's not long to learn all the tricks."

They had gathered up all the boxes and were dragging them onto the porch when their dad came out, looking for better cell reception. He nodded to them and said, "Hey!" but kept his eyes on the screen.

"I'm going to be in the show!" said Jessie.

"That's great," he said without looking up, and punching buttons with both thumbs. Jessie thought she heard him curse under his breath, but she couldn't be sure.

"And we caught a mole!" she said, hoping he would turn his attention to her. She wanted to tell him that she'd been super smooth, but she knew that was bragging, and for some reason she couldn't understand, bragging was something you were *not* supposed to do. Maybe Evan would tell her dad how good she had been at catching the mole. But Evan was tearing the duct tape off the boxes and making a pile of the rocks. No doubt she would be the one who would have to carry them back to the woods.

"It was supposed to be a rabbit!" said Jessie, trying one more time to get her dad to listen.

"Hmm . . ." said her dad, frowning and reading his screen.

"A rabbit!" Jessie shouted in frustration. Sometimes her dad was great, and sometimes it was like he wasn't even there. All of a sudden she felt again the pain of missing her mother's phone call. Why couldn't she have been home? Her mother would have asked a million questions about her rabbit traps.

"Oh, my God! A rabbit!" said her dad all of a sudden, and Jessie thought that she had finally gotten through to him. But instead he turned to Evan and said, "I completely forgot. When I was out getting the wood cut, I stopped by Petco and picked up a rabbit. It's in the trunk. Here—" He dug into the front pocket of his jeans and fished out the keys to their mother's Subaru, which he tossed to Evan. Luckily, Evan caught them. There were a lot of cracks in the floorboards of the porch, and if the keys had fallen through one, there would have been no way to get them out.

"You forgot a *rabbit?*" asked Evan, holding the keys.

His dad shrugged and waved his hand absentmindedly just as his phone rang. He turned his back on them, saying urgently into the phone, "I've been trying to get in touch with you for days . . ." And then he did curse. Loud enough for everyone to hear.

"Come on, Jess," said Evan. They hurried around the side of the house to where the Subaru was parked in the driveway. In the sun.

"You can't leave an animal in a hot trunk," said Jessie nervously. Oh, this was going to be bad.

Evan tried to open the trunk with the key, but it stuck. Ever since their mom's car got rear-ended a couple of years before, the trunk would stick. Sometimes jiggling the key worked, and sometimes it didn't. "Try popping the latch from inside," said Evan.

Jessie opened the driver's side door and pulled up on the latch for the trunk. But even though the latch popped up, the trunk remained shut.

"What are we gonna do? What are we gonna do?" The black upholstery of the car was soaking up the strong May sun. It was at least ninety degrees outside, which meant it was probably more than a hundred degrees inside the car. What was the temperature inside the trunk? Jessie imagined herself in that tight, dark, hot place and felt her heart start to race.

"Let's . . . um . . ." Evan was still trying to get the trunk to pop by jiggling the key.

"We should ask Dad. He'll get it open."

"Jess! He's the one who ditched the rabbit in the first place!"

"But the rabbit's going to *die!*" Jessie had heard about things like this happening. Dogs left in closed-up cars for even a few minutes on cool spring days. But on a day like this! She knew that furry animals had a really hard time controlling their temperature, because they couldn't sweat. They would overheat and then die.

"Look, get in the back," said Evan. "I'll see if I can get the seat to fold down and then you can crawl into the trunk from there."

Jessie and Evan jumped into the back seat, and Evan inserted the key into the lock that held the seats in place. It took a lot of wiggling and pulling, but they finally got one seat to fold forward, leaving a small rectangular opening into the trunk.

"Climb in and grab the rabbit!" said Evan. He was too big to fit through the narrow space, but Jessie was just the right size.

"But it's dark in there! And it's . . ." Jessie started to panic. What if she crawled in and couldn't get back out? What if the rabbit was loose and tried to attack her? What if it bit her face? What if she couldn't breathe?

"It'll be fine," said Evan. "I'll hold on to your leg the whole time. If anything happens, I'll just pull you out."

Jessie stuck her head into the trunk but backed right out. "I can't see anything. It's pitch-black."

"Just feel around. There's got to be a box in there." He put his hands on her shoulders. "Jessie, you have to do this. You have to be brave. I'll be here the whole time. I promise."

Jessie ducked her head inside and then eased her shoulders through the hole. There was just a little bit of light leaking through, but the far corner of the trunk was completely dark. She couldn't see a thing.

She scooted her hips through and then both knees and started inching her way forward in the dark. The air inside the trunk was heavy and hot. It made her lungs feel clogged up. The top of the trunk pressed down from above, so she couldn't crawl properly. She lay down on her stomach and reached forward with both hands. She tried to breathe normally, but it was like trying to breathe wet cotton balls.

Her hand inched forward. She felt something about the size of a shoebox. She grabbed it and pulled it toward her. As she started to back out, her foot seemed to get caught on the edge of the opening. She tried kicking, but she couldn't feel her way out.

"Evan! Evan! I'm stuck." She kicked harder with her foot. Her hands holding the box started to shake, and she worried that she would rattle the frightened rabbit to death.

"Stop kicking! I'll pull you out. Ow!" shouted Evan. Jessie could feel his strong hands grabbing her ankles and yanking. In less than three seconds she was out of the trunk, draped over the back seat, with the cardboard box in her hands.

"I don't think it's alive," whispered Jessie. She was close to tears. All the edginess of being stuck inside the trunk mixed with her worry about the poor, hot rabbit. Why had her dad left the rabbit in the trunk? How could he have left it there?

"Come on," said Evan. "We gotta look."

Evan unhooked the cardboard tabs on the sides of the box, and together they looked inside.

Chapter 10
Proscenium Arch

proscenium arch (n) the arch in a theater that separates the stage from the audience; it is often where the curtains hang

The rabbit seemed to be okay—although Evan couldn't help thinking that if Jessie hadn't said the word *rabbit* to their dad, the poor animal would have roasted alive in the hot trunk.

Jessie promptly named him Professor Hoffmann. He had snow-white fur, with streaks of gray, and a serious face, which made him look like a professor. The inside of his short, upright ears was the color of bubblegum. When Jessie and Evan ran to the back porch to tell their dad that the rabbit was okay, he looked at them strangely. "Of course it's okay. Why wouldn't it be? Why do you two always worry about everything? Your mother, too! It's like you want bad things to happen."

Sometimes bad things do happen, Evan thought, but he didn't say it out loud. He didn't want to sound as if he wasn't tough, like his dad, who had been to war and seen really horrible things.

Their dad hadn't bought any of the things you need to keep a rabbit, so Evan and Jessie did the best they could with what they had in the house. They lined a clean, large cardboard box with shredded newspaper and filled Evan's old Scooby-Doo cereal bowl with water. Jessie wanted to decorate the box, but Evan said decorations wouldn't be safe. Professor Hoffmann might eat them.

For the next two days Evan worked intensely with Professor Hoffmann and Jessie to perfect the appearing-rabbit trick. At first Professor Hoffmann didn't like going into the wooden box at all. He would kick his legs and paw the air with his forelimbs, as if he were trying to swim up and out of the box.

"He's remembering when he was stuck in the trunk," said Jessie, trying to calm Professor Hoffmann by feeding him some lettuce. She still wouldn't touch or hold him, but she liked giving him food.

"Don't feed him. He's supposed to be working," said Evan, trying once again to get the rabbit to sit still. After a few minutes they noticed that he had pooped. Jessie ran screaming from the room, but Evan just cleaned it up with a paper towel, and after that Professor Hoffmann didn't mind sitting in the rabbit box anymore.

* * *

On Wednesday, Jessie showed Evan the latest edition of *The 4-O Forum,* and Evan had to admit it was terrific.

The front-page article was all about the magic show, and it explained that this was a show with a real live rabbit and an actual stage. The stage was almost finished being built. Their dad had bought

The 4-O Forum

Special Magic Issue   All the News That's Fit to Print

Now You See It!

By Jessie Treski

This coming Monday, Memorial Day, should be renamed Magic Day, because that is the day that a magic show is coming to town. Prepare to be mystified by the Amazing Magician Evan and his Spectacular Assistant Jessie as they dazzle you with their illusions. They will do card tricks, rope tricks, and sleight of hand. Amazing Magician Evan will make a live rabbit appear out of nowhere. The rabbit's name is Professor Hoffmann. How does he do it? No one knows! But one thing is for sure: You won't want to miss this Mystifying and Magnificent Medley of Magic! Buy your tickets now!

enough two-by-fours to build a proscenium arch, and he'd also bought yards of red velvet, which they draped over the top of the arch to form curtains. Evan couldn't help wondering where his dad got so much money. And if he had that much money, why didn't he send more of it to them?

"I'm going to pass them out tomorrow," said Jessie as Evan handed back the newspaper.

"Are you sure Mrs. Overton will let you?" asked Evan. Mrs. Overton had not allowed Jessie to hand out her Valentine's Day issue of *The 4-O Forum*. Too much love stuff. "Maybe she won't because we're charging money for the show. It's like advertising."

"She won't mind. Besides, it's not just about the magic show. I've got an interview with Mr. Franks, and a word puzzle, and a huge article on the weather station data and the storm. See? The whole back page. Did you know they named it? It's called Tropical Storm Annabelle."

"Hmm." Evan didn't care much about the weather. He just hoped someone would come to the magic show. He had almost perfected the appearing-rabbit trick. It would be lousy if no one came to see it. In fact, he could use an audience right now. "You want to see me do the trick?"

"Yes!" shouted Jessie, immediately jumping onto the bed.

"Can I watch, too?"

Evan turned to see his dad, who'd been gone for the last hour, in the doorway. When had he gotten back? How long had he been standing there? It made Evan feel nervous. His dad had always been good at sneaking in and out of places, but Evan had never quite been able to understand how he did it. "One of my professional secrets," his dad always said.

Evan swallowed. He felt ready to have Jessie watch him perform—but his dad? What if he messed up? What if Professor Hoffmann tried to kick his way out of the rabbit box when he was supposed to be "gone"?

But his dad didn't wait for an answer. He walked right in and lounged on the bed, resting his head against the wall.

Evan straightened the prop table so that it was facing his new audience; he took a deep breath.

"And now, ladies and gentlemen," he said in a booming voice, "for my final illusion, I will make a rabbit—a live rabbit!—appear out of thin air before your very eyes." He waved his hand at the rabbit box on the top of the prop table. "As you can see, I have an ordinary wooden box. The box is empty." Evan opened the top of the box and waved his hand around inside to show that the box was empty. "Now, I will take this silk handkerchief"—Evan had borrowed one of his mother's scarfs, which he draped over the box so that the front was covered—"and, voilà!" He lifted the silk scarf and there was Professor Hoffmann, sitting in the box, his pink nose twitching.

Jessie clapped madly, and Evan's dad nodded his head in approval.

"That is a great trick," he said. "You performed it really well."

Evan knew he was supposed to act very casual. Magicians never lose their cool. But he couldn't help smiling. It had taken him two days to learn how to rest his hand on the box, release the secret latch with his pinkie finger, and lift the silk scarf, all in one fluid motion—as if he were doing nothing at all. He was glad his dad was seeing him perform the trick now instead of yesterday, when he'd looked clumsy and anybody could have guessed the trick.

"But . . ." His dad leaned forward. "I thought you wanted to make something *disappear* as your final trick."

"Yeah," said Evan, reaching into the box and taking Professor Hoffmann out. He liked to give the rabbit a piece of carrot every time he did the trick correctly. "But it's way harder to make a rabbit disappear than it is to make him appear."

"Yeah, I bet. That's what makes it such a great trick, right?"

"He's pooping!" shrieked Jessie, pointing at Professor Hoffmann.

"Oh, Jessie, stop making such a big deal," said Evan. "So he poops! He's a rabbit, for Pete's sake!"

"I wish he didn't!"

"Yeah, well, he'd be dead if he didn't, so that wouldn't be so great."

"A dead rabbit. That would definitely spoil the show, huh?" said their dad, laughing. But Evan didn't think it was so funny. "Hey, put the rabbit down and come see what I've got in the back of the car."

Evan put Professor Hoffmann in his large cardboard box and then he and Jessie followed their dad out to the driveway. It was starting to rain. Big, sloppy, hot drops fell from the murky gray sky, and Evan thought of Mrs. Overton's warning "to keep a weather eye out."

"What is it?" asked Jessie as the three of them pulled a long cardboard box from the back seat of the Subaru. Evan had the sudden thought that it was the size and shape of a coffin. There were five or six different labels on the box, some of them written in an alphabet Evan didn't know.

Evan pointed to one of the labels. "What kind of writing is that?"

His dad glanced at it, then back over his shoulder as he maneuvered the box up the front steps. "Devanagari, probably. At least that's what I'm guessing, since the box came from India."

"You know people in India?"

"I know people all over the world," said his dad, grunting as he pushed open the front door.

When they got the box in the kitchen, their dad carefully sliced it open with the Swiss army knife he kept in his pocket. With each slice of the knife, another side of the cardboard box fell away until they could finally see what lay inside: a rectangular wicker basket about the size of a small bathtub.

"What is it?" asked Jessie impatiently.

"Do *you* know?" he asked, looking at Evan.

"Wow," said Evan. "I've seen a picture of one of these. In Professor Hoffmann's book!"

Their dad looked at him strangely. "The rabbit has a book?"

"No! Different Professor Hoffmann," said Evan.

Evan ran his hands over the top of the basket. "It's got a fake bottom. You flip it over—" He grabbed hold of the top of the basket and turned it on its side, but the bottom stayed where it was.

"It's broken!" said Jessie, pointing at the opening.

"No!" said Evan. "That's the secret. That's how you make the person disappear, because then you unhook this other side—" He reached inside and ran his hand along the top edge of the box until he found a small metal latch and unhooked it. The side of the box fell open and covered up the missing bottom.

Jessie frowned. "I don't get it. I want to see the picture." She ran to get the book.

FIG. 301.

STEP 1: THE ASSISTANT LIES DOWN IN THE BASKET

FIG. 302.

STEP 2: THE MAGICIAN CLOSES THE LID

The second flap falls into place and looks like the original bottom. The assistant is hidden from view.

Assistant is on the ground

FIG. 303.

STEP 3: THE MAGICIAN TILTS THE BASKET FORWARD

"Look," Evan said. "Step One, the assistant lies down in the basket. Step Two, the magician closes the lid so the audience can't see. Step Three, the magician tilts the basket forward and the false bottom falls out, so the assistant is still lying there on the ground. But at the same time, the secret flap—which looks just like the false bottom—falls into place and covers up the assistant."

"I still don't get it," said Jessie. Evan could tell it bugged her that she couldn't figure out the trick.

"Here. Give me a second to set it up, and I'll show you." Evan and his dad lifted the rectangular basket onto the kitchen counter, and Evan positioned Jessie on the other side of the room so that she was looking at the basket straight on. "First you open the lid on top, and then you have a person get inside." He grabbed a bunch of bananas from the fruit basket and said, "Just say this is a person."

"Bananas!" shouted Jessie.

"Yeah, bananas, but in the trick, it will be a person. Then you close the lid and flip the box on its side." Evan turned the box over so that it was resting on its side. "Then you open the lid, and look—" The box was empty. "Ta-da! No bananas!"

"How'd you do that?" demanded Jessie.

"I told you. It's a fake bottom. The person's hidden behind the box, but the audience can't see that."

"You're pretty good, Evan," said their dad. "Now, if you ask me, *that* would be a great finishing trick for your show."

"Make *me* disappear! Make *me* disappear!" shouted Jessie.

"Where'd you even get this thing?" asked Evan. He couldn't believe his dad had found something like this. And gone to all the trouble to get it.

"I just made some phone calls," he said. "I knew what I was looking for. I've seen that trick a dozen times in Mumbai. So I called a friend or two. Actually . . ." He scratched his chin. "Six."

"So that's who you were talking to on the phone all this time? All those phone calls were for this?"

"Some of them. What do you think?"

The smile on Evan's face was so wide he thought his face might split in two. "You're the best!" he said, and rushed at his father, wrapping his arms around him.

His dad hugged him tight and kissed the top of his head. "Let's take it out on the porch, and you and Jessie can practice. You've only got—what?—four more days until the show, right?"

Together, they carried the basket out to the porch and set it up under the proscenium arch. Evan couldn't believe how real it all looked. Just like a professional magician's stage.

His father stood on the grass where the audience would be and looked carefully at the stage. "There's just one problem," he said slowly. "When I saw the trick performed, the person really did disappear. There was a trapdoor in the floor of the stage, so once you flipped the basket back up, the person slipped away and then reappeared at the back of the audience. It was amazing." He nodded his head thoughtfully. "Yeah. I think you should do that."

"Make a trapdoor?" asked Evan.

"But . . ." said Jessie. "We'd have to cut a hole in the porch."

Their dad nodded his head. "That's what I think

we should do. To really sell the trick."

"Mom would kill us!" said Evan.

"Why? The whole porch needs to be replaced anyway. Look at it!" He walked up to the edge of the porch and started pulling on one of the rotting floorboards. "Honestly, it's a miracle your mom hasn't been hauled into court yet."

"Stop that!" said Jessie. Her eyes were wide as she watched her dad pull apart the porch, and she was jumping nervously from one foot to the other.

"You know what?" said their dad. "I'm going to make some calls and line up a carpenter to put on a new porch. That way, we'll have all the repair work scheduled before your mom even gets home. It'll be like a present we give her! A terrific surprise. She'll love it." As gracefully as a cat, he leaped onto the porch and walked into the kitchen, leaving Evan and Jessie staring at each other silently.

"Evan?" Jessie sounded scared.

"What? Don't look at *me!* He's the grownup." Evan knew in his heart that his mom wouldn't like any of this, but—a trapdoor! How cool was that? "Besides, we'll end up with a new porch."

"I don't want a new porch!" Evan knew that Jessie didn't like change of any kind. She liked things to stay the same.

"Well, we're getting one, so get used to it. Like Mom says, 'Adapt and evolve,' Jess."

Their dad opened the sliding door to the kitchen and stuck his head out. He had his cell phone to his ear, and he was grinning. "Hey, look. When your mom calls tomorrow, don't tell her about the new porch. I want it to be a surprise, okay?" Before either Evan or Jessie could answer, his attention returned to the phone. "Yes. I want to get an estimate . . ." He disappeared back inside the house, closing the door behind him.

"What are we gonna do, Evan?" asked Jessie.

Evan looked at the Indian basket. "Practice. A lot."

Chapter 11
Heckling

heckling (v) calling out insults or rude comments from the audience in order to disrupt a performance

By noon on Thursday, Jessie had already counted thirty-six kids who said they were coming to the magic show on Monday. She'd handed out *The 4-O Forum* in the morning, and right away students—some of them even fifth-graders!—had asked about tickets. *Maybe we should have charged more,* thought Jessie. She was excited about the money—thirty-six dollars—but she was also starting to get that hard-to-breathe, thumping-heart feeling that sometimes ran through her like a freight train.

Here it was—Thursday afternoon—and they still hadn't practiced the disappearing trick even once. They'd spent all yesterday afternoon cutting the hole in the porch. It was a big deal; they had to avoid the thick boards that ran underneath the floor-boards, because that's what held the whole porch up. If they accidentally cut through one of those, the porch might collapse.

"That would be a showstopper!" their dad had joked, but Jessie didn't laugh.

First they'd cut in one spot, but then they decided to put the trapdoor in a *different* spot, and by the time it got dark and they had to stop, they hadn't finished even one hole.

When Jessie got home from school, the hole *still* wasn't finished, even though their dad had promised he would work on it while they were at school. Instead, Evan was sawing away at the floorboards using the old hacksaw. His hair stuck to his forehead in big, sweaty clumps, and his hands were bright red from gripping the saw so hard.

"It's not done yet?" asked Jessie.

"What does it look like?" snapped Evan. "You think it's so easy, you try it."

"I'm not allowed to," said Jessie. "Neither are you. Where's Dad?"

"In there." Evan waved at the house. "On the phone. Again."

"Maybe he's getting you another basket. Or another rabbit," said Jessie. She didn't like it when Evan seemed angry.

"No. It's all work stuff. Very *important* work stuff." What did it mean when Evan talked like that? Jessie couldn't remember. Her mom had explained it to her, but now she wasn't sure. It was one of those confusing things where people said one thing but meant another. She wished her mom were here to explain it to her.

"I get to talk to Mom first today, remember?"

"She's not calling. She texted Dad and said she was trapped in a meeting and couldn't get away. She'll call tomorrow."

"But I want to talk to her today! I want to tell her about the newspaper and how many kids are coming to the show." Jessie knew she was whining, and she knew she should stop. People really do not like whining. This had been explained to her many times by both her mom and Evan, though Jessie could never really understand why. What made whining worse than regular talking?

Evan stopped sawing and looked off into the woods behind their house. "Yeah, me too," he said in a soft voice. He tapped the blade of the saw against the wooden floor. Then he tossed the saw onto the porch and said, "C'mon, let's go inside and have a snack. Dad bought ice cream. Three flavors!"

Jessie was still trying to decide between chocolate chip and peppermint stick when their dad wandered into the kitchen, talking on his cell phone. He leaned against the jamb of the sliding glass door and stared out into the backyard. "So you're saying there's movement? And you're sure?" There was a long pause while the person on the other end of the line talked. Jessie could hear the murmuring of a voice, but she couldn't make out any of the words. She decided to take a scoop of both kinds of ice cream. Mom wasn't here to tell her not to. Her dad kept talking. "And you can't get anyone to talk? Anyone?" The voice on the other end of the phone made its humming noise, and then her dad said, "Okay. I'll figure something out." Then he hung up the phone and stuffed it into his back pocket.

No one said anything for a minute. Jessie wanted to talk, but she had that sudden feeling of danger that she couldn't identify. Something inside said *keep quiet,* even though she couldn't figure out why.

"What's going on out there?" asked her dad, pointing to the half-cut hole in the porch floor.

Evan shrugged. "Nothing, I guess."

"Well, that's not an attitude that will get you very far in life," said their dad. He went outside, and in a moment Jessie could hear the sound of the saw rasping against the rotten wood.

"Why don't you go help him, Evan?" asked Jessie, noticing that Evan's bowl of ice cream was empty.

"He doesn't need me," said Evan. "There's only one saw." Even so, he wandered outside a moment later, and when Jessie finished eating her ice cream, she walked out to the porch and saw that the hole was complete.

"Now we just have to cover it so no one can see it's there," said their dad. "Go grab that little area rug from your mom's office. It's the perfect size."

Evan and Jessie looked at each other. There were a lot of rules in the Treski house, but the number one rule was: no taking *anything* from Mom's office.

"Oh, c'mon," said their dad. "It's not like it's some Persian rug. I bought that thing from Home Depot about ten years ago. Go get it!"

"Can we practice now?" Jessie asked on the stairs as they lugged the small rug down. She wanted to be sure she could do the disappearing trick perfectly. There was no way she was going to mess up in front of thirty-six kids from school. Including fifth-graders!

"Yeah," said Evan. "But it's pretty easy. I mean, all you have to do is lie still in the basket and then jump through the hole when I say the magic words. There's not much to it."

When they had the rug positioned over the hole, Evan told Jessie to stand to one side of the basket. Their dad jumped off the porch and stood where the audience would be.

"Ladies and gentlemen!" Evan said in his stage voice. "For my final illusion of the day, I will perform the Amazing Disappearing Trick!"

"Yeah, right!" shouted their father obnoxiously. "You couldn't make an ice cube disappear in a microwave!"

"What?" said Evan, looking confused. He stared at their dad.

"I'm heckling you," said their dad. "You have to be prepared in case you have some rude person in the audience who starts shouting things during your show."

"They're my friends. They're not going to be jerks," said Evan.

"You never know. It's important. If you want to be the best, you have to know how to handle yourself in any situation. It's like the military. They run every drill they can think of so that the soldiers are ready for anything in combat." He put his hands to his mouth and shouted out, "You call that a rabbit? I've seen potatoes with more energy!"

"Dad! Cut it out!"

Their dad shook his head. "You kids have to get *tough*. You're too soft living here in the suburbs. C'mon. You're Treskis. You have to learn how to handle the rough stuff."

Jessie had no idea why her dad was saying all these mean things to Evan. Why would anyone do that? Why were people mean on purpose? It didn't make any sense to her. But she knew she wanted it to stop.

"Be kind and do your work!" she barked. That was the classroom motto in 4-O. Their teacher, Mrs. Overton, had hung that motto over the door so that they would remember it at all times. Jessie thought it was pretty good advice. "And let us do *our* work!" She wasn't sure if *she* was being kind at that moment, because she was yelling, but sometimes strong words were the only ones that worked.

"Now, that's what I'm talking about!" said their dad. "Tough! Way to go, Jessie. You could be in the army!"

Jessie smiled and jumped up and down once, waving. This was almost as good as getting applause from an audience.

Evan kicked the basket. "Can we do this thing already?" He scowled at her. "Ladies and gentlemen. And now, for my final illusion, I will perform the Amazing Disappearing Trick. Behold! A basket with four strong sides." Evan knocked on each side to show that the basket was solid. "And now, I lift the lid and ask my assistant to step inside." He motioned for Jessie to step into the basket. It was like getting into the bathtub. Jessie didn't much like taking baths, but she wasn't afraid of them.

"And now, my assistant will lie down."

Jessie immediately lay down.

"And I will close the lid."

The lid came down on top of her, blocking out the sky, the trees, the light. All of a sudden Jessie felt as if a hand were pressing on her chest, squeezing all the air out. She kicked with both legs against the lid, and it popped back open.

"Jessie! What the heck? You can't do that! You have to lie still."

"It's too dark!" squeaked Jessie, jumping up like a puppet on a string. She wanted to get out of that basket as fast as she could.

"Wait, wait!" said Evan. "It's not dark. It's a basket. Look. There's a lot of light coming through. You could probably read a book in there!"

"It's too dark! It's too small! There isn't any air!"

"It's a basket! There's tons of air." Evan looked frustrated. "Why are you being so weird?"

"I'm not! It's not safe."

"Problems?" asked their dad, calling from his place in the audience.

"No!" shouted Evan. He turned to Jessie. "Look. Just try lying down. I won't put the lid down, okay? Just lie down and get used to it."

Jessie trusted Evan more than anyone in the world. Even so, her heart was pounding inside her chest as she slowly lowered herself into the basket, holding on to the sides as if she were in a very tippy canoe. As soon as she lay down, her stomach started rising and falling.

Evan squatted down next to her so that his head

was just visible over the side. "Okay?" he asked in a quiet voice. "Not so bad, huh?"

Jessie nodded just slightly, afraid that if she did more than that, she might throw up.

"So do you think you can let go of the sides?" he asked, almost whispering. "Just put your hands down inside the basket?"

Jessie used her brain to tell her fingers to uncurl slowly and come to her sides. *I'm safe. I'm safe. I'm safe,* she kept telling herself.

"You're doing great, Jess," said Evan. "Now listen. I'm going to leave the lid open, okay? But I'm going to tilt the box so you can practice slipping out, just like we'll do during the show. Ya ready?"

Jessie nodded again. It helped having the lid open so she could see the sky—and especially Evan's face. She knew that as long as Evan was looking right at her, nothing bad could happen. Still, she could feel sweat beading up at her temples and dribbling into her hair. *Just stop it!* she told her sweat glands angrily. *You have no reason to be scared!*

Evan tilted the basket forward so that it seemed

to fall away from her, and there she was—lying on the porch with nothing around her! Free! She was out of the basket and free! She felt as if she'd just escaped being buried alive.

"I did it!" she shouted. "I did the trick!" She scrambled to her feet, feeling that she could suddenly breathe again.

"You're not supposed to stand up, Jess! You're supposed to go through the hole and hide under the porch," said Evan. "Let's do it again. And this time, I'm going to close the lid, okay?"

"Do you have to?" asked Jessie, frowning.

"The trick doesn't work if the audience can see you the whole time."

Jessie knew he was right. If she wanted to be a magician's assistant, she would have to be closed up in that basket. That was her job. But the thought of being shut up in the basket—it really was exactly like a coffin!—made every muscle in her body want to *get away,* just the way the mole they'd caught had tried so frantically to escape the rabbit trap.

Jessie didn't want to let Evan down. He was counting on her. And she really wanted the audience to applaud for her. She was good at lots of things in school: she always got one hundred percent on her math worksheets, she was the fastest reader in the whole grade, and her desk was always the neatest in her class. But no one applauded those things. Evan got lots of applause and cheers when he played basketball. He even had trophies to display in his room. What would it feel like to have people applaud for *her?*

Mostly, though, Jessie wanted her dad to see her do something extraordinary—disappear right before his eyes!—and then clap the loudest and the longest of anyone in the audience.

Jessie stepped into the basket. Immediately her heart started to pound and her lungs felt twisted up, so she couldn't get a good breath in. *It's okay. It's just a basket. You can get out anytime you want.* Her legs began to wobble as she lowered herself down, down, down. *It's just a basket. You can just push it off. It's okay.* She pulled her hands in close to her sides and watched as the lid began to close. *Evan's here. He won't let anything bad happen to you. It's okay. You're safe. You're safe. You're safe.*

The lid closed with a soft creak, and Jessie could hear Evan slide the wooden pin through the leather latch. Now she was locked inside, and a wild panic took hold of her and made her shake like a leaf in a storm. *Locked in. Can't get out. No way out. No air. Too dark. Can't breathe. Can't breathe!*

And then something was fighting and clawing and letting out the most terrible sound she had ever heard. The basket was banging all over the place, hitting her in the arms and legs, and Evan was shouting at the top of his lungs, but she couldn't tell what he was saying, because everything was muffled and far away except for the horrible screaming of the wild cat, which sounded as if it was right inside her own head.

And then the basket flopped off of her, the false bottom opening up so that she was lying out in the open on the porch, staring up at the wide blue sky, which looked as if nothing had happened at all. She rolled over onto all fours and pushed herself up.

"Jeez, Jessie!" said Evan. For some reason he was sitting on the porch, as if he'd been knocked over. Jessie stood panting, trying to get her breath back.

Then her dad was there, looking at her closely with some kind of strange expression on his face. Jessie couldn't tell if he was angry or sad or worried—or all three.

"Are you okay?" he asked her, but it wasn't the kind of face that went with those words. It was not the kind of face her mother would have had if she'd been there.

Jessie looked from Evan to her dad and knew that they knew something she didn't. She hated that feeling. But not as much as she hated the feeling of being locked inside the basket. Nothing was worse than that.

"I want to call Mom," she said.

Evan stood up slowly and began to set the basket back the way it was supposed to be. "She can't talk today, remember?"

"I don't care. I want to talk to her," said Jessie. The back of her throat felt prickly, which meant she was about to start crying. Jessie hated crying. It was messy and gross and left her with a stuffed-up nose. Plus, she did *not* want to cry in front of her dad.

"Hey," said her dad. "How about sending her a

text? You can use my phone, all right?" There was still something strange about the way he was looking at her. And his voice sounded weird, too. It was as if he were talking to someone he didn't even know.

Her dad punched buttons on his phone, then handed it to her. "All set," he said. "Just type what you want to say."

Jessie turned her back on Evan and her dad. She was good at typing, and it took her less than three seconds to type what she wanted to say to her mom.

Come home.

Chapter 12
Grand Finale

grand finale (n) the last part of a performance, typically the most exciting spectacle of the show

"Take a break," Evan said to Jessie on Friday afternoon. They had been running through the show for the past hour, and they were both hot and tired. The outdoor thermometer read ninety-two degrees, but the air was so sticky and thick that it felt like a hundred. To make things more difficult, odd gusts of wind would occasionally blow through, upsetting the prop table, sending the cards flying into the air, then disappearing, leaving the air even heavier than before. Evan knew Jessie was doing her best to keep everything in place, but she only had two hands.

And then Professor Hoffmann started to act

strange. He kept hopping around the edges of his large cardboard box. Twice he kicked over his water bowl. And whenever Evan picked him up, he trembled.

"It's the barometric pressure," said Jessie. "We measured it today at school. It's dropping because of the storm."

"Rabbits don't have weather stations!" said Evan crossly. He was frustrated because he hadn't had a chance to practice the grand finale.

"Animals can tell, though. They can sense changes in air pressure, and they can hear infrasound. Professor Hoffmann *knows* that Annabelle is coming."

"Well, if he's so smart, does he know when Dad's going to get off the phone?"

"No," said Jessie thoughtfully. "I don't think so."

"Jess, that wasn't a real question!"

"Then why did you ask it?" asked Jessie. She was setting up the cards for the first card trick exactly the way he had taught her, but the wind kept blowing the cards off the table. "We should practice inside," said Jessie.

"I can't practice the grand finale inside! I need the hole in the floor, remember?"

"Well, practice everything else inside and then, when Dad gets off the phone, practice the grand finale outside."

"But he hasn't gotten off the phone for the last three hours! He's *never* going to get off the phone." Evan needed his dad because after Jessie's panic attack yesterday, his dad had offered to be the one to climb into the basket and disappear. At first Evan had thought it wouldn't work. His dad was a whole lot bigger than Jessie, and Evan didn't think he could fit inside the basket. But it turned out that if his dad scrunched his legs in a particular way, he could just barely squeeze inside with the lid closed.

Evan had felt so glad—so grateful—that his dad was willing to do the trick in Jessie's place. The show wouldn't be ruined! He could still perform the Amazing Disappearing Trick.

But after walking through the illusion once yesterday, their dad had been too busy to rehearse any more. "I've got it, Evan," he had said. "It's not that complicated. We can practice more tomorrow if you want."

But when tomorrow became today, his dad had been even busier. Something important was happening somewhere in the world that had their dad's full attention.

"C'mon," said Evan. "Let's take all this stuff inside. Maybe we should take the curtains down, too," he added, eyeing the long red velvet drapes they had hung over the proscenium arch. Every once in a while the drapes would flap vigorously in the wind before dropping back to their usual droopy positions.

"No," said Jessie. "The storm isn't going to get us. It's tracking west by about two hundred miles." She sounded disappointed. Jessie liked to see things firsthand.

Evan looked at the curtains. It would be hard to get them down without help. Even though Evan was the second-tallest boy in fourth grade, he still wasn't tall enough to take down the curtains without a ladder. And their dad? Evan knew better than to ask for his help.

Evan's mother wasn't a whole lot taller than he was, but they made a good team. He could hold the ladder and she could climb up—or the other way around. Whenever there was a tough job to do, they figured out how to do it together: installing the air conditioners, moving the refrigerator, digging up the dead lilac bush.

Evan heard the screen door slide open. He looked up, and there stood his father in the doorway with the phone to his ear and a manila folder in his hand. He waved the folder at the two of them. "Take-out," he said. "You pick the place."

"I don't want take-out again!" said Jessie. "I want real food."

"Sorry, Tootles. I don't have time to cook dinner."

"Do you even know how?" Jessie asked. Evan knew she wasn't being sassy. She just had never seen their dad cook. But Evan was older, and he could remember a time when their dad would cook huge pancake breakfasts on sleep-in Sundays. That's when their mom got to sleep late and their dad took care of them. It hadn't happened often, but Evan could remember.

"I'm an amazing cook," he said, waving the folder again, "but not tonight." Then his attention turned back to his phone call, and he said, "Yes, I'm waiting. No, that isn't the reason . . ." and he dropped the folder on the porch and went back inside.

*　*　*

The pizza was heavy and greasy and sat like a lead ball in Evan's stomach. He'd eaten four slices, which was two more than usual. It wasn't even about being hungry; it was just about wanting to eat.

"I feel like I'm going to barf," said Evan.

"That's because you ate like a pig," said Jessie. It was her turn to do the dishes, which was lucky for her because there were just two plates and two cups. Their dad had grabbed a slice and a napkin and headed into their mother's office. Rule number two in the Treski household was absolutely, positively no food in Mom's office.

"Actually," said Jessie, "pigs don't overeat. They eat just until they're full and then they stop. And a pig can run a seven-minute mile. Also, pigs can't sweat. That's why they roll in the mud to keep cool."

Normally Evan would have argued about the seven-minute mile—a pig couldn't run that fast!—but he was too busy thinking about his mother coming home tomorrow. She would be home in time for lunch! No more greasy pizza.

He decided to go upstairs and ask his dad if he and Jessie could ride to the airport with him. The door to his mother's office was open a crack, so Evan pushed on it and went in.

His dad was sitting at his mom's desk with his back to the door, typing on the computer. Evan looked over his dad's shoulder and saw a picture of a big jet airplane on the screen. His dad was typing information into a form, and when he heard Evan behind him, he held up one hand as if to say, *Hold on a minute.* He clicked the mouse one last time, then turned to Evan.

"Change of plans," he announced. "Did you know there's a storm coming up the coast?"

"Yeah, Dad. We've been studying it in school all week. Jessie showed you the article she wrote."

"That's right! Good article. Okay, so you know, and Jessie knows. That's good. So look, I need to head out tomorrow as soon as your mom gets home. I'm going to be lucky if I can catch a flight out before the airports start to close. Atlanta's already closed, and they'll close JFK by morning, which means I might need to go west to fly east . . ." Evan's dad turned back to the computer screen. He began to scroll through the long list of flights. "Or if I can get an earlier flight to London . . . squeak out before the storm hits, and then . . . I can connect in Dubai, and from there—well, I'll figure that part out later. There are ways . . ." His voice trailed off as he stared at the screen. Evan felt as if his dad had forgotten that he was even in the room. The silence between them opened wide like a canyon.

"So, you're going to miss the magic show," Evan finally said.

There was another moment of silence. Evan could hear the rain beginning to fall on the roof above their heads, and he thought about the red curtains hanging on the stage. They would get soaked. He hoped they wouldn't be ruined.

Evan's dad turned around to face him. "I'm

really sorry. I am, believe me. I was looking forward to it. But hey, you don't really need me for that disappearing trick. You can do it with the rabbit, or how about one of your friends? I bet one of them would love to be in your show."

"But you said you would." His dad had promised. Evan looked around the room. This was his mother's room. Everything in it felt as if it was a part of her. The books on the bookshelf, the stacks of papers, the desk, the chair, even the tiny attic window tucked under the eave of the roof felt like her window. How many times had he come into this room, and there she was—sitting at her desk, working. It was one of those things you could count on.

"Sorry, man. Something's come up. Something big. I can't tell you what, but a lot of lives are at stake, and I, well, I just have to be there. Trust me on that. I don't have a choice."

"You're not the only reporter in the world." Evan kicked the toe of his sneaker against his mother's file cabinet. It made a dull thud, punctuating the silence.

Evan's dad leaned forward, as if he was going to share a secret. "No, but I'm the best." He flashed his million-dollar smile at Evan. Evan didn't smile back.

Evan remembered the day his dad left. Evan was just seven years old—almost eight, and Jessie was six and a half. It was in May, the same month as now, except that the day had been cold. Evan remembered because he'd run outside when he realized what was happening and hidden himself high in the branches of the Climbing Tree, and then he'd wished he had a sweatshirt because the air was cold against his skin.

His dad had come out in the backyard looking for him, but Evan had kept quiet. He was up high enough that you would need to stand right under the tree to see him. Evan pulled his legs up and wrapped his arms around the trunk of the tree, hoping to be invisible.

His dad kept looking for him until he finally spotted him, and then he climbed right up the tree. His father, slow and heavy, didn't know all the good branches where he could put his feet. Evan could climb up that tree even with his eyes closed. But his dad lumbered up, finally sitting on the branch just below Evan's.

He'd started a long speech about how sad he felt and how leaving was something he had to do.

"You're too young to understand this now," he said. "But when you're older, it'll make sense, I promise. Every one of us has a purpose, a reason we're put on earth. There's a path for each of us, and you have to follow your path. Otherwise, your life is just wasted."

Evan didn't understand what these words meant or why his dad had to leave.

"I love you and Jessie and your mother very much, but this"—he raised his chin slightly in the direction of the house—"this isn't the life I was meant for. This isn't my path. This is your mother's way. It's just not right for me."

"But can't you go and then come back?" asked Evan. "And we'll still be a family?"

"Hey," said his dad, "we'll always be a family. I just won't live here anymore."

"But why?" asked Evan. It didn't make sense to

him. It was home. Why wouldn't you want to live at home?

"Look," said his dad. "This is complicated stuff. Very grown-up stuff. You'll understand it when you're older, okay?"

And suddenly it was Evan's fault. For not being older, for not being more grown-up, for not understanding things his dad needed him to understand. It was all his fault. And he still didn't understand it.

"I've gotta go now," his dad had said. "Your mom is . . . um, well. She's pretty upset right now. You're going to have to help her through this, okay? I know you will. You're a Treski, and Treskis are tough, right?"

And then he'd climbed down from the tree and left. Evan heard the taxi pull into the driveway, the trunk door open and close, and then the opening and closing of the passenger door. The taxi had skidded on some gravel pulling out, and there was the long, slow fading sound of the car's engine. Then nothing but silence.

For two hours Evan had sat in the Climbing Tree, the cold creeping into his bones until he didn't think he could make his fingers work to grip the branches on the way down. But finally he had climbed down and walked into the house, and that had been that.

Now, here in the tiny attic office, the temperature was the opposite. The room was like a small oven, closed up and fiery. Evan felt as though every breath he took was sucking the last of the oxygen out of the shut-up space. And instead of going numb, he felt stung by his father's words, his skin itchy and hot.

"All joking aside," his dad said, "I really do have to go. It's important work I do, Evan. You know that. Remember what I taught you? What John Stuart Mill said? That the press is the last security against a corrupt and tyrannical government. And it's true. Without reporters like me, the governments of the world would do terrible things and no one would know to stop them. Hey, I'm keeping the world safe, Evan. For you and Jessie and your mom. That's the truth."

There was a long silence then, and Evan felt as if his dad was waiting for him to say something. As if his dad *wanted* something from him.

"I suppose we should *thank* you," said Evan slowly. "Thank you for leaving us. Thank you for *never* being around when bad stuff happens. Thanks, Dad! You're the *greatest!*"

"Don't be a smart aleck, Evan." His dad shook his head, disappointed. "It doesn't make you sound smart."

"Well, I'm *not* the smart one in the family, am I?" Evan felt as if his words were a wave pouring out of him. There was no holding it back. "I bet you wonder how you ended up with a dumb kid like me."

"Evan, you're a terrific—"

"I bet you don't even tell people you have kids. All those people in India and Afghanistan and Iraq! You probably don't even tell them that you have a family. And that's good, because you *don't!*"

"Evan, lots of families are separated like we are."

"No! No one is like us. Those dads live nearby, and they see their kids all the time. But you go away for months and months, and sometimes we don't even know where you are."

"My work is different. I can't broadcast where I am all the time. Sometimes I'm in hiding with the soldiers. I can't put them at risk to send you a birthday text. C'mon, Evan. You're old enough to understand that! Some things are more important than a phone call from your daddy."

Standing, Evan was taller than his dad sitting down, and now he crossed his arms and looked down severely. "Family comes first. That's what Mom says." Suddenly Evan wished his dad would leave, right that minute. They didn't need him! They were fine without him. Better than fine!

Evan walked out of the office without saying another word. There was nothing left to say. When he got to his own room, he hung up the Locked sign, closed the door, and didn't come out for the rest of the evening.

Chapter 13
Patter

patter (n) a soothing, repetitive sound; a magician's continuous talk during a performance that lulls an audience so they won't notice something that's happening onstage

When Jessie woke up, it was raining—a soft patter on the roof—and the first thing she thought of was Professor Hoffmann. She wondered if he could hear the rain down in the basement and if the sound had made him nervous in the night. He seemed to be a very nervous rabbit to Jessie. The second thought that popped into her head was that today was the day her mother was coming home. Finally. Jessie couldn't wait.

She slipped out of bed and straight into her slippers. She didn't like walking barefoot, even in the house. Then she quickly made her bed.

The window to her bedroom was open a couple of inches, and rain was blowing through and onto the floor. She slammed the window shut, then headed downstairs.

In the basement, Professor Hoffmann was nervously circling inside his large box. Jessie squatted down and put her head close to the edge, hoping that the sight of a giant human head peering down on him wouldn't make him even more scared.

"There's nothing to worry about," she said in a matter-of-fact voice.

But Professor Hoffmann kept going around in circles. This was one of the things that Jessie didn't like about animals. You couldn't explain things to them. They just didn't understand. Especially rabbits. Still, she liked Professor Hoffmann. He was a good worker. He had practiced his tricks and learned to sit still and never kicked her when she put him in the rabbit box.

She checked his food tray and refilled his bowl with fresh water. Then she headed upstairs to the kitchen to wash her hands and get some breakfast.

On the kitchen counter was an envelope, and on the outside of the envelope were the words "Evan and Jessie." Jessie frowned. The handwriting was her father's, all capital letters and a little sloppy. Why would he write them a note? Maybe he wanted to sleep in and was telling them not to wake him up until it was time to go to the airport and pick up their mom.

Jessie quickly washed her hands, then picked up the note and hurried upstairs. Evan was still sleeping, but the note seemed important.

She hesitated a moment outside his door. Now that Evan was almost eleven, he had started sleeping in on the weekends. When they were younger, he and Jessie had both gotten up early whether it was a school day or not.

The Locked sign stared her right in the face, daring her to knock—and face the consequences. She knocked.

"Go away!"

"But it's important!"

"You always say that!"

Jessie paused and thought about the last half dozen times she'd knocked on Evan's door. "But it *is* always important." She didn't knock without a good reason.

"Ugh. Come in."

Jessie hurried in and jumped onto Evan's bed, climbing over his stretched-out legs to position herself with her back against the wall. She liked being able to see everything that was going on, no matter where she was. Without a word, she handed Evan the note.

When he saw the handwriting, he sat up quickly and tore open the envelope. He pulled out a piece of Mom's nice stationery, the kind she used for formal letters and thank-you notes. Jessie crowded next to Evan so they could read the letter at the same time.

Jessie read the note twice. Then she read it again, just to make sure she hadn't missed anything. But there was nothing to miss.

> HEY, KIDDOS!
>
> HAD TO LEAVE EARLY
> BECAUSE OF THE STORM.
> MOM WILL BE HOME SOON.
> KNOCK 'EM DEAD AT
> THE SHOW.
>   LOVE,
>   YOUR DEAR OLD DAD

"He's gone," she said at last.

"Yep," said Evan, crumpling up the note and throwing it into his trash can. "Just like always."

Jessie pulled her knees up to her chin and thought for a minute. Evan was wrong. This time had been different. He had stayed a really long time. Days and days. But in the end, he *still* left. "Why?"

Evan shrugged. "I don't know." Then he lay back down, as if the conversation were over. Jessie wondered if Evan was about to kick her out of his room, but he didn't say anything, so she figured she was allowed to stay. She looked at the rows of basketball trophies that Evan kept on the bookshelf above his desk.

"Is it because he doesn't like us?" asked Jessie, but in her head she was wondering, *Is it because he doesn't like* me? Any dad would be happy to have a son like Evan—basketball star, most popular kid, talented magician. But she wasn't so sure what her dad thought of her.

"He likes us okay," said Evan. "He just likes other things more."

"What other things?"

"Work. Travel. Living out of a suitcase. Pretty much everything. I bet if Dad made a list of the most important things in his life, we'd be like number fifteen. After his cell phone, that's for sure."

Jessie studied Evan and could tell he was feeling bad. First of all, he wasn't looking at her when he talked. Second of all, his voice didn't sound the way it normally did. Third of all, he hadn't kicked her out of his room, even though he clearly wanted to sleep.

And then she wondered what *she* was feeling, and she decided to do her Feeling Check. Very quietly, she began to run through her list. "Am I happy? No. Am I sad? No. Am I scared? No. Am I angry? No—"

"Je-e-e-ss . . ."

"I'm doing my Feeling Check," she said.

"I know what you're doing. Can you do it inside your head?"

"No. It only works out loud."

"Ugh!" Evan said, covering his head with his pillow to block the sound. But still, he didn't kick her out of his room, which was very unusual for him, and Jessie couldn't figure out what that meant.

"Paint a picture," she whispered to herself, and closed her eyes. The first thing that flashed in her mind was the picture of the little baby spiders in *Charlotte's Web* that float free like balloons at the end of the book. She knew it was supposed to be a sad moment in the story, but she always thought it was wondrous.

Jessie opened her eyes. "When is Mom getting home?"

Evan looked at the clock on his night table. "In about four hours."

"Okay. Then I'm going to go watch cartoons." Usually Mrs. Treski didn't allow Saturday-morning TV, but since there wasn't a grownup around to ask . . . "You wanna come?"

"Nah. I'm going to sleep some more."

Jessie wandered out of the room but came back just a few minutes later.

"Evan! You need to come see! Quick!" She yanked on the blanket covering him and tried to grab his T-shirt to pull. "I'm serious. Get up!"

He must have heard the panic in her voice, because he jumped out of bed. "What?" he asked as they ran downstairs.

"The storm is coming! Here! It's not tracking to the west. It's headed straight for us! And it's not a tropical storm anymore! It's a hurricane!"

In the family room, the TV was on, with a large map of the East Coast of the United States filling the screen.

"It's on all the channels. No cartoons. Just the weather!" said Jessie. "Listen!"

". . . highly unusual to have a Category 1 hurricane on the East Coast this early in the season. We're going to see sustained winds of up to eighty miles per hour. The real damage, though, is going to come in the form of flooding. As soon as the storm makes landfall later tonight, we're going to see heavy, heavy rain . . ."

"I want to call Mom!" said Jessie loudly.

"We can't call Mom," said Evan. "She's on a plane. And besides, we don't want to tell her that Dad isn't here. She'd *freak*."

"There's a Category 1 hurricane coming!" shouted Jessie "We don't have anything we need! The house is going to get blown to pieces. This is why Professor Hoffmann was acting so weird! He knew! He knew all along!"

"Relax!" barked Evan. "Just calm down. Mom is going to be home in a couple hours. Let's just turn off the TV—"

"No!" shouted Jessie. "We need to know what's happening, even if it's bad."

"Then you have to calm down! 'Cause I can't deal with you flipping out, okay?"

"Okay, okay. I'll calm down. I promise."

They sat side by side on the couch in front of the TV and tried to make as much sense as they could of what the TV reporters were saying. Jessie was right: the weather was on every channel, and it was big news. There had never been a hurricane in their area before Memorial Day, so all the newspeople were saying it was a one-in-a-million storm. The storm was expected to make landfall sometime around midnight and continue through all of Sunday. The airport was closed, and the governor had declared a state of emergency.

"Evan! The airport is closed! What about Mom?"

"Maybe she's already landed," said Evan, looking at the clock. "Let's . . . let's eat breakfast. I'm hungry."

But Jessie couldn't eat anything except chocolate pudding, and only a few spoonfuls of that. Her stomach felt as if it was ready to turn itself inside out, and her head was achy and heavy.

At ten o'clock the phone rang, and Jessie put her hands over her ears to stop the sound from splitting her head in two. Evan picked it up on the third ring.

"Oh, hi, Mom!" said Evan. Jessie crowded close to the receiver so she could hear too. Usually Evan would have pulled the phone away, but this time he let her listen in.

"Bad luck, guys," said their mom. "I tried to be sneaky and get an early flight out to beat the storm, but the plane they put me on had engine trouble, and now I'm stuck in Cincinnati, of all places!"

"What do you mean, 'stuck'?" shrieked Jessie.

"No, it's okay! Don't worry. I'm fine. Just let me talk to Dad now, and then I'll fill you in on all the details."

Jessie clamped both of her hands over her mouth and pressed hard. She wanted to scream, *He left! He left us!* but Evan was giving her a look that meant *Don't you dare say a word!* and Jessie knew to keep her mouth shut.

"He had to go out," said Evan.

"Out? I guess to get stuff for the storm. But I've been trying to get him on his cell phone and he doesn't pick up."

"Well, you don't need to worry," said Evan. "Everything's fine. We're fine. We already had our breakfast, and now we're just watching some TV." Talking to his mom like this made him think of his magician's patter—the way he talked onstage to keep the audience from noticing what was really going on. Jessie shook her head vigorously, but she kept her mouth closed tight.

"TV? In the morning?" said Mrs. Treski, then paused. "Okay. When Dad gets back, have him give me a call. If he can. My battery is running low. Honestly, it's been one thing on top of another. I can't remember the last time I had so many things go wrong all at once. But you guys are fine?"

"Yep," said Evan.

"All right," said their mom. "I'm doing my best to get home, but there's not a lot of information at the moment. I heard the airport at home is closed, so I don't think there's a chance I'll make it until after the storm passes. Tell Dad to check to make sure you have batteries. And fill the bathtub with water, just in case. Jess, are you okay?"

"Yes," squeaked Jessie. "I want you to come home."

"I know, sweetie pie. I'll be home as soon as I can. Are you having fun with Dad?"

Jessie started to cry. Evan pulled the phone away.

"Yeah, we've been having a good time," he said. "So, we'll see you soon!"

After Evan hung up the phone, Jessie really started to wail. Evan put his hands on her shoulders and marched her into the laundry room, where their mother had hung up an old-time poster that was popular in England during World War II. The bright orange poster showed the British crown with the words KEEP CALM AND CARRY ON emblazoned underneath.

Their mother said the British were an inspiration to the whole world. They had survived months and months of bombing by the Germans and still went about their daily business and kept the country running. When she felt overwhelmed by laundry, she liked to think of their courage.

KEEP CALM
AND
CARRY ON

"C'mon," said Evan. "We're fine. Look at us. At least no one's dropping bombs on us."

It was true. Everything *was* fine—for the moment. Jessie stared at her mother's poster, then said, "We need to get all the things in my newspaper article."

Be Prepared!
What You Need In An Emergency
By Jessie Treski

Big storms like Annabelle take big preparation.
Here's a list of everything you need to survive a big storm.

- Water, one gallon per person per day for three days
- Food, a three-day supply of nonperishable food
- Battery-powered or hand-crank radio and extra batteries
- Flashlight and extra batteries
- First-aid kit
- Whistle to signal for help
- Dust mask to help filter contaminated air
- Plastic sheeting and duct tape
- Moist towelettes, garbage bags, and plastic ties
- Wrench or pliers to turn off utilities
- Manual can opener for food
- Local maps
- Cell phone with charger (solar or hand-crank)

It was a long list. Some of the things were easy to gather, like flashlights and batteries, which their mother always kept on hand in case of power failures. But some of the things were harder to figure out. Three days' worth of nonperishable food? They checked their cabinets for canned goods, but most of it seemed pretty gross. Cold white beans? Stale crackers? There were sardines, but that made both of them gag. Cereal was okay, but they'd have to eat it without milk if the power went out, and Jessie hated the sandpaper feeling of dry cereal.

And they didn't have a battery-powered radio or a cell phone, let alone one with a hand-crank charger. Hopefully, if they lost power, it would only be for a couple of hours.

They spent most of the afternoon discussing—and arguing about—how to get everything on the list, not to mention where to keep it all. Jessie thought they should take everything up to the attic in case of flooding. Evan thought they should put everything in the basement, in case the roof blew off. In the end, they left a huge pile of food, blankets, batteries, duct tape, plastic bags, local maps, screw drivers, pliers, and paper towels in the middle of the kitchen floor. It looked like a garbage heap, but Jessie knew it might save their lives. Then they brought in everything from the porch—the soaking wet curtains, the rug, the scrap wood—and put all of that in the garage.

The rain continued steadily all afternoon. Around dinnertime the wind picked up. Jessie could hear it whistling under the eaves, swirling around the house as if it were trying to pry loose a board and find a secret way in. Outside, the trees in the woods creaked and groaned, and a shutter that was loose on the back of the house started to bang. The late-afternoon light faded, and darkness draped itself over the house. She watched old reruns on TV, trying not to think about the long night ahead.

At nine o'clock, Jessie was brushing her teeth when the power went out.

"Evan! Evan!" she shouted, spitting toothpaste into the pitch-black darkness.

"I'm coming! I'm coming!" he called back. "Keep your pants on!"

Jessie felt for the edge of the sink, repeating,

"Keep calm and carry on. Keep calm and carry on." It was just darkness. There was nothing in the dark that wasn't there in the light. There was nothing to be afraid of. But the sudden plunge into black made her heart race and her brain freeze up.

"Where the heck are you?" Evan's voice came from the hallway, and then there was a bouncing circle of dim yellow light and Jessie could see the faded outlines of things. Evan's face looked ghostly in the feeble glow, but at least it was Evan. "You've got toothpaste all down your front," he said, pointing the flashlight beam right at her heart.

Jessie did a quick rinse and spit, and then the two of them went down to the kitchen to arm themselves with flashlights. Jessie wanted two: one to use and one to keep as a backup.

When she got up to her room, she realized something much worse. There was no night-light. Jessie always slept with a night-light. It helped keep bad dreams away.

"You can use a flashlight," said Evan. "Just keep it switched on."

"It'll run out. In the middle of the night." And

that would be the worst. To wake up in the middle of the night. Alone. In the dark. With a hurricane raging outside. "Can I sleep with you?"

Evan made a face. "You kick."

"I know. I'm sorry. I can't help it."

"I can't sleep with you kicking all night. And there isn't enough room. We're both too big." He shrugged, as if there was nothing he could do about that.

The wind outside howled, and there was the sound of something ripping away from something else, followed by a loud, rattling bang.

Jessie shook her head. "I can't sleep alone without my night-light." Evan would have to think of something.

"We'll share Mom's bed. It's bigger."

This was a great idea. Jessie hurried ahead of Evan, hoping to claim the side that her mom slept on. But once she had buried herself under the sheets, she noticed that the bed didn't smell like her mom.

"It smells like Dad," she said.

"Yeah," grumbled Evan, climbing in on his side.

"Good night, Evan."

"Night, Jess."

They both lay silent for several minutes. Jessie felt herself tense up every time the pitch of the wind rose. Something was scraping against the window, and Jessie told herself over and over that it was just a tree branch from the maple in the side yard. Still, it sounded like a demon trying to break in.

"Evan, are you awake?" she asked.

"No," he answered, and that made her giggle. "We're going to be okay, Jess. Just go to sleep, okay?"

"Okay," said Jessie. "I'll try not to kick you."

"That would be great."

Then they both fell asleep, first Evan, then Jessie, while the hurricane came closer and closer.

Chapter 14
Disorientation

disorientation (n) a technique whereby a magician confuses his audience, often with rapid patter and flourishes, so that they don't notice a gimmick or sleight

When Evan woke up at dawn, he didn't know where he was. He'd been dreaming of an elephant caught in a trap, and the cry of the elephant howling in pain was still in his ears.

But this wasn't his bed. And there was a strange sound—something was rattling. Something was trying to break out or break in. Evan sat up. The room was nothing but shadows. His T-shirt was plastered to his back, and the bedsheets were twisted around his legs. He couldn't figure out where he was.

And then something kicked him, and he realized that Jessie was sleeping next to him, and suddenly he remembered. The howling was the wind, and the rattling sound was the windows of their old, drafty house, shaking and raging against the storm.

Evan got out of bed to get a drink of water. The wind was louder than anything he could remember hearing. He could feel the house shake under his feet. The windows were rattling so much he thought they would shatter. Occasionally something thudded against the house, and Evan wondered what it could be.

He looked out the window. Through the smudgy daylight he could see the rain blowing sideways against the house. It looked as though someone had turned on the sprayer of a giant garden hose and was aiming it right at the window. There were no streetlights or house lights on. But as his eyes became accustomed to the dim light, he began to see certain shapes. Several large tree limbs were down, and one of them was lying across the road. Part of the fence in front of the house across the street was knocked flat, and the gate had blown up against the mailbox on the corner. Strangest of all, something was stuck high up in the tree right in front of their house. At first Evan couldn't figure out what it was: some big, round object with polka dots painted on it. Finally he realized it was one of those plastic kiddie pools, wedged in the branches of the tree, thirty feet off the ground. As he turned away from the window, he saw two lawn chairs chasing each other down the middle of the street.

Evan climbed back into bed. Jessie was snoring loudly, but he could hardly hear her over the roar of the storm. Something banged outside. The house creaked like a ship tossed on open water. *It's going to fall apart,* he thought. *It's too old and broken-down.* What would they do then? He struggled to settle his mind, and after what felt like hours, he fell asleep.

* * *

It was a sound like an explosion that yanked Evan back awake. At first he thought he hadn't slept at all, but then he saw that there was daylight outside—a dark murkiness, but daylight nonetheless. The sound was so loud, it even woke Jessie, who could sleep through an army invasion.

"What was that?" she shouted, looking at Evan with wild eyes. The sound of the outside storm seemed even louder than before, as if it was rushing into the house through a gaping hole.

Evan and Jessie hurried out of their mother's room and followed the noise of the storm. When they looked in Jessie's bedroom, they couldn't believe their eyes. A large tree limb was sticking right through the wall and lay across Jessie's bed. There was a hole about the size of a car door, and rain was pouring through it, soaking the bed and the floor. Chunks of plaster from the ceiling had fallen on top of the mess.

Evan looked at Jessie, expecting her to flip out, but the expression on her face was very still. Jessie didn't like *anything* to mess up her room, not even one tiny bit. What was she thinking now?

Jessie pointed at her bed. "If I'd slept there, I'd be dead," she announced, like a reporter stating a fact.

"Nah," said Evan, who didn't even want to think

about that. But what if Jessie *had* been in her bed? What would he have done then? To shake the thought loose, he asked, "What tree is it?"

They carefully crossed the room to the hole in the house and peered out.

"Oh, Evan! It's the Climbing Tree!"

It was true. The Climbing Tree had snapped in half, and the top of it had crashed into their house. Evan felt a stab of pain—it was almost as if someone had died. The Climbing Tree was more than just a place to hang out. There were times when it had felt like Evan's only friend in the world. Times when he'd needed to get away—from the house, from Jessie, from the fighting between his mom and his dad, from his own impatience or frustration or confusion. And the Climbing Tree had always welcomed him, held a place for him, and let him just be, without asking one single thing in return.

Evan felt like raising his head to the sky and howling. But he couldn't. Jessie was here, and she was looking at him. Waiting.

"Look," he said. "We should probably . . . um, do something . . ." He pointed to the open gash in the house. He just wanted to go into his own room and close the door and bury himself under the covers on his bed. He wanted someone—anyone—to take charge. And once again, that old fury rose up in him. His *father* should be here.

But he wasn't. He'd left. Disappeared when they needed him most. And there was no point in getting mad about that *now*. There were things that needed to get done. Things that couldn't wait.

He thought about Pete and the repairs they'd made to Grandma's house after the fire. He remembered Pete's words. Instructions, strong and clear.

"We need to stop the rain that's coming in," Evan said. "It's going to wreck the house."

"Wreck the house?" shouted Jessie, waving at the tree in her bed.

"Well, even *more*," said Evan. "Water is a house's worst enemy." It was as if Pete were standing there. *You gotta keep the water out. That's job number one.*

Evan sent Jessie down to the garage to grab the plastic tarps that their mother kept there.

"How are we going to hold the tarps in place?" asked Jessie when she came back upstairs.

Evan looked at the hole. "Nails," he said decisively.

Jessie's eyes grew wide. "Nails? In the wall? Mom is going to kill you if you do that!"

"Jess, look at this! It's a disaster. I don't think a few nails in the wall are going to make it any worse!"

So they pounded about twenty nails into the wall, securing the tarp at the top of the hole. Jessie had the bright idea of hanging the bottom of the tarp over the tree branch and out the hole so that the water would run off outside. Even so, a fair amount of water was still pushing its way in around the sides of the tarp, which flapped in the vicious wind. The tree was also acting like a straw, drawing the water in from outside and dumping it on the bed. Jessie, who was good at figuring out how things work, had an idea. She and Evan wedged the two smaller tarps between the tree and the mattress, and then they shaped the tarps so that there were two gullies in the plastic. The water that poured on top of the tarp gathered in the gullies and ran off into two buckets that Jessie positioned on the floor. It was sort of like the marble tracks that she and Evan sometimes built.

"That's the best we can do," said Evan.

"We just have to remember to change the buckets, because they're filling up pretty quick," said Jessie. It was true. There was already almost an inch of rainwater in each bucket. How could the sky hold that much water?

They carried the heavy, sodden towels they'd used to wipe up the puddles down to the laundry room and piled them on the dryer. No electricity, so there was no way to dry the towels. In the kitchen, they each poured a bowl of cereal, but decided not to open the refrigerator door, in the hopes that the food inside would stay cold enough until the power came back on. They sat in the dim room, away from the sliding glass doors in case any more tree limbs fell, and ate their bowls of dry cereal.

"Do you think this is as bad as it's going to get?" asked Jessie. Evan had been wondering the same thing. Without a battery-powered radio, there was no way to get news of the storm. No TV, no Internet, no phone. They were completely cut off—as if they were living in Antarctica, with no connection to the rest of the world.

"Maybe we should go to the Kapours'," said Jessie. The Kapours were their neighbors on the right.

"No," said Evan. "We don't need them. We're fine." He knew this wasn't true. There was a hurricane raging outside and a hole the size of a bathtub in their house! But he didn't want to tell anyone that their dad had left them alone. That their mom had gone to California and not come home when she promised. He didn't know what would happen if anyone found these things out, but he didn't want to risk it. It was better to stay where they were and ride out the storm.

"But what if . . ." said Jessie. "What if . . . the house falls in on us? Or . . . a window breaks and there's glass everywhere. Or what if . . . the basement floods and water starts to come up the stairs . . . ?"

Evan looked at Jessie, and he could see that the same thought was forming in her head that was taking shape in his. A picture of water seeping into the basement, creeping up, inch by inch.

"Oh, Evan," said Jessie, running to the basement door. "We left Professor Hoffmann down there. All alone!"

"Wait!" said Evan. "We need a flashlight!"

He ran upstairs to his mother's bedroom and grabbed a big Maglite, the strongest flashlight they owned, then grabbed a second one for Jessie. When he got back down to the basement door, Jessie was already feeling her way downstairs, gripping the railing and testing each step with her foot. Evan shined the light ahead of them, but they both stopped short before reaching the bottom step.

The basement was completely flooded. Water leaked in through the cracks in the cement, streaming down the concrete walls like waterfalls. Evan guessed the water was about a foot deep, since the bottom two steps of the staircase were completely submerged.

"Where *is* he? Where's his box?" screeched Jessie. Her flashlight beam was jiggling all over the basement, making the room seem to jump before his eyes.

"I don't know, Jess," said Evan. "Just hold steady.

Stop flashing your light everywhere. Here. You look on that half and I'll look on this half." There were so many things floating in the water: old sneakers and a box of light bulbs and a plastic car. Evan pointed his beam of light at a half-inflated beach ball and Jessie's old coloring books. Two Easter baskets floated by, bobbing in the water like toys in a bath-tub.

But then Jessie shouted, "Look!" and pointed to the corner where her flashlight was aimed. Evan swung the beam of his light, too, and they both saw. Something floating on the surface of the water.

It was Professor Hoffmann's cardboard box, torn apart and flattened, soaked through with water—and empty.

Chapter 15
Disappearance

disappearance (n) a magic trick in which an object, person, or animal seems to disappear

Jessie ran upstairs to get her high rain boots, then sloshed through the rising water in the basement, calling out, "Professor Hoffmann! Where are you? It's us. Come out!" She looked on all the shelves, thinking that perhaps he'd jumped up, trying to escape the flood. That would be a natural instinct in an animal: to seek higher ground. But Jessie looked on every shelf in the basement, and there was no sign of the rabbit.

Evan, who didn't have rain boots, stayed on the stairs and held the flashlights. But after ten minutes he said, "Jess, we can't stay down here. The water's getting higher, and I think there's yucky stuff in it. See?" He pointed to the water near the furnace, and Jessie could see that there was an oily slick on the surface. "Come on."

At the top of the stairs, Jessie pulled off her boots. "Where do you think he went?" she asked, but in her mind, she knew the answer. Professor Hoffmann had drowned, and when the storm ended and the water emptied out of the basement, they would find his small, limp body, and he would never do a magic trick again.

Jessie had never loved an animal before, but she loved Professor Hoffmann. She loved him because he was quiet and predictable and simple and didn't need much. Sometimes he was calm, and sometimes he was nervous. But mostly he just wanted to eat lettuce and occasionally a radish. He needed water and his box cleaned out from time to time, and you could count on him to do his job. He was an easy rabbit to understand.

She tried not to think too much about what he had gone through at the end. She told herself that rabbits don't feel fear the same way humans do. But

as the morning stretched on and the storm continued to rage, Jessie grew more and more frightened
herself, and she couldn't help thinking that Professor Hoffmann had felt some of the same things she
was feeling now.

*   *   *

"Evan, the buckets are overflowing!" Jessie shouted,
looking in her bedroom for the fifth time that day. It
was incredible how fast they filled now that the rain
was coming down harder than ever.

"Give me a second," Evan called back. "There's
another leak in the kitchen!" The ceiling in the
kitchen had started to drip in the afternoon, and
Evan and Jessie were on steady patrol, checking
each room for new leaks. So far there was one in
their mother's bedroom, one in the bathroom, and
three in the kitchen. The only room that had managed to stay completely dry was the family room,
and that's where Evan and Jessie had moved their
supplies to and where they would hunker down between patrols.

"This is hard," said Jessie at one point. She was

trying to open a jar of pickles. Jessie loved pickles, but her mom never let her have more than two at a time because eating too many gave her a stomachache.

"I can do it," said Evan, reaching for the pickle jar. He was eating tortilla chips dipped in cold hot-fudge sauce.

"That's disgusting," said Jessie matter-of-factly.

"Actually, it's not half bad," said Evan, returning the pickle jar with the lid loosened. "Don't eat more than two."

"I know, I know," said Jessie. She didn't like touching food with her hands, particularly wet, cold food, so she used a fork to stab a pickle and fish it out of the jar. As she crunched, she thought of Professor Hoffmann and said again, "This is hard."

"What?"

"Everything. This whole storm. It's a lot of work." *And a lot of sadness,* she thought.

"Yeah. I'm tired."

"Do we have to stay up all night? Because of the buckets?" asked Jessie.

"I guess. Unless the storm stops. Do you think it's slowing down?"

They both listened to the howling of the wind and the slapping of the rain against the windows. Jessie had almost gotten used to it, the storm had been going on for so long. It felt like days and days. "No," she said finally. "I don't think it's slowing down at all."

"I wish we had a radio," said Evan for about the fourth time that day. "I just want to know what's going on."

Jessie finished her second pickle, thought about taking a third, then put the lid back on the jar. She hadn't been very hungry all day, but she knew she should eat something to keep up her strength. She reached for the last Lorna Doone in its plastic sleeve. "You want to split it?" she asked.

"Nah. I already had about ten of them." Evan leaned back and closed his eyes. Jessie thought he was going to fall asleep right there on the couch. But then he sat up and said, "I better go check the basement. To see if the water's gotten higher."

Jessie hadn't gone back down to the basement since the morning. She couldn't bear it. But Evan had checked every hour, counting the number of steps that were still untouched by the water. At last check, the water had risen so high that only ten steps were still above water. What if the water reached the top step and started to spill into the kitchen?

Jessie took a deep breath. "I'll come with you," she said. The thought of going down those stairs, descending into the murky darkness and all that swirling water, made Jessie feel as if she were lowering herself into a deep, dark well.

Plus, it wasn't just a basement anymore. It was a graveyard.

"You don't have to," said Evan. "I can go by myself."

But Jessie insisted, so they rounded up every flashlight they could find—seven in all—and turned them all on. Evan carried two under his arms and two in his hands, but Jessie carried all three of hers in a bundle. She wanted a good, strong light for whatever lay ahead. Before opening the basement door, Evan stopped.

"Jess, if the water's really high, I think we have to go get help."

"You mean, we have to tell someone that Dad left us?"

Evan nodded his head.

Saying it out loud sounded so awful. *Dad left us.* Jessie wondered if he would be arrested. Were there laws against leaving kids in a hurricane? There should be!

"Why did he do that, Evan?" Just because their dad loved his job didn't mean he couldn't love them, too. Did it?

"I don't know." Evan sounded really tired. His whole body slumped. Then he straightened up suddenly. "But I hate him! I hate him for leaving us—again! And for the storm—"

"The storm isn't his fault," said Jessie seriously. You couldn't blame a person for a hurricane. That was an act of nature.

"It *is* his fault. He's a grownup. He should have known. He should have *cared!*"

Jessie didn't know what to say to that. She didn't like it when Evan got angry at their dad. It made her feel as if somehow *she* had done something wrong.

She looked at Evan. "He's just . . . Dad."

He shook his head. Jessie couldn't tell if she had said the wrong thing. But Evan's face had lost its angry look. He just looked tired again. "Oh, c'mon," he said. "Let's check the basement."

Jessie was glad that Evan was going first. If this was a horror movie, now was exactly the moment when a zombie would jump out and attack them. She could almost hear the sound of scary music playing. Jessie stepped carefully on the narrow wooden steps. Her hands were full of flashlights, so she couldn't hold on to the railing the way she usually did. She was trying to point the flashlight beams down on the stairs so she could see where she was stepping, when all of a sudden Evan yelled, "Look!"

Jessie's first thought was *zombie!*, and she instinctively reached for the railing to turn and run. The flashlights slipped from her hands. She lunged, trying to catch them before they hit the stairs, but her foot slipped and she fell forward, crashing into Evan and then tumbling into the cold, dark water below.

Chapter 16
TnR

TnR (n) abbreviation for Torn and Restored, a special kind of trick in which the magician cuts, rips, or breaks something into pieces (a string, a card, a stick) and then makes it whole again

"I'm drowning! Evan, I'm drowning!"

Evan splashed down into the dirty water and grabbed hold of Jessie. "You're not drowning! Just stand up!" One of Jessie's flailing arms smacked him across the face, and Evan fell back, dunking himself in the sludgy water. He came up sputtering, not sure where Jessie was. The basement was as dark as night, with just a dribble of daylight coming from the open door at the top of the stairs. Evan could hear Jessie splashing and gasping for air, but he couldn't see her. Then he felt a sharp kick underwater. He reached in that direction and grabbed something, pulling it up to the surface. "Jessie!" he shouted. "Stop it! The water isn't that deep. Just *stand up!*"

Jessie wrapped both arms around his body, as if letting go of him would mean the end of the world, but he could feel that she had set her feet on the basement floor and was standing on her own. She was coughing hard, but it sounded to Evan as if she was breathing okay.

"C'mon," he said. "This water is gross." He half dragged her to the stairs and helped her walk up and out of the water.

"Why did you yell 'Look'?" asked Jessie, still coughing.

"Because! The water's *lower*. It's gone down two whole steps." It was good news, but nothing sounded like good news now that he was soaking wet.

When they reached the top of the stairs, Jessie stopped and sat down. "My socks are squishy wet." Evan knew that Jessie didn't like to have wet clothes on, especially wet shoes and socks. She'd been this way ever since she was little.

He sat down on the step below her and helped her untie the soggy shoelaces and then pull off each shoe and peel the soaking-wet socks off her feet. Jessie carefully tucked each sock inside her shoe and then tied the wet laces together so that they made an easy-to-carry shoe bundle. She looked at Evan. "Professor Hoffmann is dead."

Evan nodded. "I know. And the Climbing Tree is gone."

Jessie looked at the water below them. "And Dad left us."

Evan nodded again. He pushed the bottoms of his pajama pants up past his knees. The wet fabric was sticking to his legs like octopus tentacles. He'd lost both slippers when he'd plunged into the water, and it was too dark to see if they were floating or if they'd sunk.

And that's when Evan realized the worst thing of all: they'd lost all the flashlights. Every single last one of them. They were all underwater, and there were no more in the whole house. How would they make it through another night without flashlights?

"This is the worst day ever," said Jessie. "And that is *not* hyperbole."

Evan nodded. There was nothing else to say.

"Do you think it's over?" asked Jessie.

Evan pointed to the steps below. "The water's going down."

"But it's not over yet," said Jessie.

"It's mostly over," said Evan.

"But not completely. The rain hasn't stopped."

"Yeah, but the worst is over," said Evan, starting to feel a little annoyed that Jessie wouldn't just let it go.

"The wind is still blowing. Another tree could fall."

"But it probably won't."

"I'm just saying . . ." said Jessie.

"Stop!" said Evan, exasperated. "We survived a Category 1 hurricane all by ourselves, and that makes it one of the best days of our whole lives!"

Jessie was silent for a split second; then she raised both hands over her head. "We're Treskis, and we're tough," she crowed. "Okay, it's a good day." She stood up. "But I swallowed dirty water, and I need to go brush my teeth and gargle."

"Good idea," said Evan, who was eager to get out of his wet T-shirt and pajama pants. "And then, let's open the freezer and grab the ice cream, really quick. Even if it's soup, we can still eat it. All of it!"

"Dibs on peppermint stick!" shouted Jessie as she raced up the stairs and into the kitchen.

* * *

By the end of the afternoon, the storm was definitely winding down. The wind still gusted from time to time, like a child after a temper tantrum who lets out an occasional howl just to remind everyone of the fury that has passed. The rain, too, slowed down until it was nothing more than a steady drizzle. Evan couldn't believe there was any rain left to fall.

When it started to grow dark, Evan and Jessie discussed the idea of lighting candles. Their mother had several decorative candles for special occasions, and Evan knew how to strike a match, although he wasn't allowed to do it without a grownup present.

In the end, though, they decided to just get through the night in the dark.

"If we burned down the house, on top of every-thing else," said Jessie, "Mom would just kill us."

Evan agreed. Besides, at this point, walking around the house in the pitch darkness seemed like no big deal. After what they'd been through, it was hardly worth thinking about. Even Jessie didn't seem to mind the dark as much. "It's like being backstage in a play, waiting for the curtain to go up," she said.

Just before going to bed, they emptied the drip buckets into the bathroom sink one more time, and Evan felt confident that they would make it through the night without the buckets overflowing. The rain had slowed to a gentle patter, the perfect noise to listen to as they fell asleep.

* * *

The next morning, the sun was blinding. It sliced through the window, cutting across Evan's eyeballs and yanking him awake.

His first thought was *buckets,* and he hurried out

of bed to make sure there wasn't a second flood covering Jessie's bedroom floor. But each bucket had barely an inch of water in it, and all the dripping had stopped. In every room Evan walked into, the sun poured in through the rain-washed windows. The world had never looked so dazzlingly bright and new.

When Jessie woke up, they ate crackers and peanut butter and apples. Evan peeled the skin off the apples for Jessie and cut them into slices. Jessie carefully spread the peanut butter onto the crackers and pressed them together to make sandwiches.

"I wish we had pancakes," said Jessie, carefully eating over a plate to catch the crumbs. Crackers made a lot of crumbs.

"Eggs and bacon," said Evan, licking his fingers to catch the oozes of peanut butter.

"Waffles!"

"Omelets!"

"Mom's coffee cake!"

They both fell silent for a moment, and then Jessie asked, "Do you think Mom will come home today?"

"If she can, she will," said Evan, knowing that this was true. But he also knew that if she didn't make it home by sundown, they were going to have to get help. Their flashlights were gone and they were almost out of food. They couldn't go on like this any longer.

"Do you think the stage fell down?" asked Jessie.

"I don't know. Let's look," said Evan, grabbing a handful of peanut butter cracker sandwiches.

It was the first time either one of them had stepped outside in two days, and Evan felt like an alien landing on a strange planet. Some things were familiar, but some things were completely weird.

The backyard was covered in fallen branches. Not just a few. Dozens of broken tree limbs lay scattered all over the lawn. There was also a big plastic trash can that Evan didn't recognize, and a patio umbrella. High up in the branches of one of the trees was a yellow tricycle. Dangling from another tree was a man's raincoat.

But the strangest sight of all was the Climbing Tree, which looked as if it was growing backwards out of the house. It stuck out of the side of the house and slanted down to the place on the trunk where it had snapped, almost as though the house had grown an arm and were reaching greedily for something in the woods. Evan thought of a trick he could do where he cut a rope into four pieces and then made it whole again. It was called Torn and Restored—or TnR—and really good magicians could do it with just about any object: a card, a piece of cloth, even a stick. Evan wished he could perform a TnR on the Climbing Tree.

"What a mess!" said Jessie enthusiastically.

Evan had to agree. The storm had done its job well. No halfway effort. You had to give it credit for that. "This is really going to bum Mom out," he said. "We should clean up as much as we can."

Jessie was already picking up the smaller branches. She liked making things neat, putting things in their place. Evan retrieved the big plastic trash can—might as well make use of it until its owner came to claim it—and they spent the next half hour filling it with sticks and carting them into the woods. It made Evan sad to think that some of these sticks were bits and pieces of the Climbing

Tree. Even worse was the picture that came to mind of how workmen would take it away. He imagined a bulldozer and chain saws. Evan hoped he would be at school when the workmen came.

"Hey! Hi!" Evan turned to see Megan Moriarty coming around the house and into the backyard. She was smiling and waving, then stopped suddenly. "Whoa! There's a tree sticking out of your house!"

"Actually," said Jessie, "it's sticking *into* the house."

"Well, you've got us beat. All we have is two missing shutters and some bricks that fell off our chimney. Plus, my dad's leaf blower is up in a tree!"

Evan pointed out the tricycle and raincoat hanging from the trees in their backyard. Then Megan noticed the stage and asked, "Are you still going to do the show?"

Evan looked at Jessie, who looked down at her feet. "There are some problems," he said. "I don't think we can do it." He felt his heart sink.

On top of everything else, there would be no magic show. He saw Jessie's eyes start to fill up.

"But you have to," said Megan. "I already sold tickets."

"What?" asked Evan.

"Jessie gave me the tickets she printed up, and some kids asked if they could buy them on Friday so they wouldn't have to wait in line. And I said yes. So they gave me their money and I gave them tickets."

Evan noticed that Jessie had stopped crying. Anytime money was the subject, Jessie perked up. "Oh, I don't think anyone would come, anyway," said Evan. "They're probably cleaning up and stuff."

Megan frowned. "Salley's coming. I saw her riding by my house this morning, and she said she's definitely coming. And the little kids who live next door to me are coming. I told their mom I'd walk them over."

Evan shrugged. "I guess we'll just have to tell them there's no show and give them their money back. Right?"

"What a shame," said Megan. "All that money! I got two dollars a ticket, you know."

"Two dollars a ticket!" shouted Jessie. She looked at Evan.

Wow. Two dollars a ticket. He wondered how many people would come. Maybe there'd be even *more* people because of the storm. Especially if no one had electricity. What else was there to do?

Evan pointed at the porch. "We don't even have the stage set up . . ."

"I'll help," said Megan. "And Salley will, too. I think everyone just wants to get out of the house! It's been, like, two days!"

Evan turned to Jessie and tilted his head to one side. Could they really do it? Put on a magic show just hours after a Category 1 hurricane? He knew that Jessie's brain was running through five different possible scenarios and coming up with the right answer.

"We should do it," she said solemnly. "And we'll dedicate the show to Professor Hoffmann."

Chapter 17
"The Show must Go On"

"The show must go on" (expression) An old phrase in show business that declares that no matter what troubles or obstacles exist, the show must be performed for the waiting audience

Each trick was better than the last. Jessie couldn't believe how good Evan was. He started with some sleight-of-hand tricks—making a coin disappear from his hand and then making it reappear behind Jessie's ear. And even though Jessie knew exactly how the trick was done, it still fooled her. Evan was that good.

After that, he did his TnR, where he cut a rope

into four pieces and made them come together into one piece. Then he did his Cups and Balls routine, placing a red rubber ball underneath one of three cups and making it appear under a different one. Next he made three balls appear, and then all three disappeared!

The audience applauded wildly, even though they had to stand because the ground was wet. There had to be at least fifty people watching the show. Almost half of the kids from 4-O had shown up, and there were lots of littler kids from the neighborhood and school. Jessie spotted a whole group of fifth-graders. And there were even a few sixth-graders. Sixth-graders!

Jessie took a bow after each trick. Evan may have been the magician, but she was the one responsible for setting up the props, and so far, she hadn't made one mistake. Twice Evan had whispered to her, "Good job!" and she knew she was as good an assistant as he had hoped for.

Next Evan began his card tricks. He started with Out of This World, then Finding Four Aces, then

Order from Chaos, and finally the Mixed-Up Kings, which was still Jessie's favorite. For each one, she set up the deck of cards just the way it needed to be done, and each trick worked perfectly. It's true what Evan had said: the assistant was the most important part of the show. Well, maybe he hadn't said *exactly* that, but something close.

It was toward the end of the last card trick that Jessie started to feel a little flippy-floppy in her stomach. She had made a promise to Evan, and he was counting on her. Her dad had broken *his* promise to Evan, and Jessie was determined not to be like her dad. But would she be able to do it? Or would she ruin the whole show?

"And now, ladies and gentlemen," Evan said in his booming stage voice, "for my second-to-last trick, I will make a rabbit appear in this empty box!"

Jessie carefully placed the rabbit box on the prop table, just as Evan had taught her, so that the front of the box faced directly out to the audience. She had already hidden Peter Rabbit inside the box behind the secret wooden panel. As she put the box on the table, she felt a pang of sadness. Peter Rabbit was made of soft material, but his fur wasn't silky or warm like Professor Hoffmann's.

Evan did a great job building up the crowd's excitement. First he knocked loudly on all four sides of the box. Then he lifted the tablecloth on the prop table to show that there was nothing underneath. Then he opened the lid of the box and waved his hand around inside to show that the box was indeed empty.

"And now, I will simply place this scarf over the box and lightly tap it once with my magic wand"— Evan tapped the box and then whisked away the scarf—"and there is the rabbit!"

The stuffed toy Peter Rabbit was in the box, lying on its side, still wearing its blue coat and holding a carrot. Jessie reached into the box and held up the rabbit for everyone to see.

"Hey! That's not a real rabbit!" shouted Scott Spencer from the audience.

"It's a toy!" called out one of the younger kids from the neighborhood.

"Well, he still made it appear out of thin air!"

shouted Jessie, annoyed that the audience wasn't applauding. It was a good trick!

"Where's Professor Hoffmann?" asked Megan. Everyone in 4-O knew that Evan and Jessie had a real rabbit named Professor Hoffmann.

"He's on vacation!" said Jessie. "You should all applaud now."

The audience applauded, but they weren't particularly enthusiastic. They had expected to see a real rabbit, and all they got was a toy.

That was when Jessie realized that the final trick *had* to be the best of the show. Everything depended on her.

"And now, ladies and gentlemen, for my grand finale, I will . . . make my very own assistant . . . disappear!"

"Yeah, right!" shouted Scott Spencer. "Are you going to use a *toy* again?"

"Quiet!" yelled Jessie. Her dad had been right. You needed to be prepared for hecklers. Being onstage wasn't as easy as it seemed.

Evan and Jessie carried the Indian basket out onto the stage, placing it directly in front of the small rug that covered the hole in the porch. Jessie could feel her heart start to speed up. Her chest felt tight, and it was hard to draw in a deep breath.

"You see before you an ordinary basket—four sides, a top, and a bottom."

"Is there a toy rabbit inside?" called out Scott Spencer.

"Be quiet, Scott," said Megan, and several people in the audience added, "Yeah, be quiet."

Evan stared at Scott. "Why don't you come on-stage and look for yourself? If you *dare*."

Everyone in the audience turned to look at Scott, who looked as though he didn't quite know what to do. Evan stood casually on the stage, as if he didn't have a care in the world, but Jessie was nervous. If Scott came up and discovered the fake bottom, the trick would be ruined.

"Huh! Why would I be afraid to go up there?" said Scott. He walked up to the front, full of swagger. Jessie knew this was Scott's way: he always tried to look bigger than he was.

"Go ahead," said Evan, gesturing to the basket. Jessie couldn't believe what a cool customer Evan was. He acted as if there was nothing in the world to be worried about.

Scott slapped at all four sides of the basket, then raised the lid and looked inside. *Please don't let him lift it. Please don't let him lift it,* Jessie repeated in her head. She was thinking it so loudly, she worried that her brain might broadcast her thoughts to the whole audience. *Stop thinking that!* she told her brain.

Scott walked around the entire basket once more, as if he was trying to think of another way to test it. Then he stopped and gave it a swift, hard kick—but the basket just slid a few inches across the porch. It held together.

"It's good," said Scott grudgingly. And right then, Jessie realized that Scott had sold the trick for them. He had made the basket more real, more believable than anything Evan or Jessie could have done.

"And now, my assistant will step inside the basket!" announced Evan. He waved both arms as if he were signaling a plane to land, and then he looked at Jessie.

Jessie had been in a lot of tight spots with Evan. Last summer they'd fought a war over lemonade.

Last fall they'd put Scott Spencer on trial. Last winter they'd had to find their grandmother who was lost in a snowstorm and fight two bullies who were doing mean things to a helpless frog. And there were all the times before the divorce, when she and Evan had sat in the Climbing Tree, waiting for their parents to stop arguing.

Jessie looked at Evan's face. It seemed as if he was trying to say something to her with just his eyes. But what? Jessie could never figure out what people meant by the looks on their faces. She needed words, and sometimes even those didn't make sense to her.

But Jessie could replay everything that Evan had said to her in the past, and she did that now, hearing inside her head, *You can do this! You're doing great! Don't worry, I'm here.*

Jessie stepped inside the basket. She felt her insides turn to liquid and drip down into her feet. There was a strange whooshing sound in her ears, and at first she didn't realize that Evan was saying, "And now, my assistant will lie down in the basket."

Jessie lowered herself into the basket, laying both

hands over her chest, as if she were dead. The sky was blue. She could hear a chain saw buzzing somewhere. A bird flew overhead.

And then the lid closed on her. The basket became dark. Her vision narrowed, corkscrewing in on itself until she couldn't see anything except two small circles directly in front of her. A large hand pressed on her chest, squeezing all the air out of her lungs, and the whooshing sound got so loud that she couldn't hear anything else. It was like the time she'd been playing in the high surf at the beach and somehow had gotten trapped under a raft that was riding a wave. She'd been pushed underwater, unable to breathe, unable to see, unable to hear anything except the pounding sound of the water as it swallowed her up.

Her legs wanted to kick, kick her up to the surface. *No!* she told herself. *You're not underwater. You're in a basket.* She tried to breathe, to prove to herself that she could. A ribbon-thin drizzle of air squeaked into her lungs.

You can do this! she told herself. *You survived a*

Category 1 hurricane without any help from a grownup. You're doing great! Don't worry, Evan's here. She kept her legs still. She waited to be able to breathe again.

And then the basket lifted away, and she was left lying on the porch in the open air, staring up at the blue sky that seemed to surround her. No one in the audience could see her, though, because the tricky false bottom of the basket was hiding her from view.

She was about to shout *I did it!* when she remembered that they were right in the middle of the trick. That thought got her brain going again, and Jessie remembered that she needed to be quick. She needed to be smooth. She couldn't just lie there.

She rolled quickly onto her side, tucking her legs in so that she was as small as possible. Lifting one corner of the small rug, she flipped it over so that the hole in the porch was exposed. Then she quietly dropped herself down into the hole. Evan was talking very loudly to the audience, building excitement for the next part of the illusion. As he circled the basket, he neatly flipped the rug back in place with his foot so that the hole was covered again.

Jessie, meanwhile, was under the porch, and it was gross down there! She had to crawl on her hands and knees, which was nasty because the ground was muddy and there were slimy wet leaves and all kinds of bugs, not to mention sharp rocks that bit into her skin. She tried to be quiet, but it was difficult. Luckily, she didn't have far to go. The part of the trestle that her dad had cut away and then covered again (a secret door!) was just ten feet from the hole Jessie had dropped through. She had to get through the secret door and then sneak around to the side yard and into the woods so that she could reappear at the back of the audience just as Evan waved his magic wand. She didn't have much time.

But when she got to the cutaway trestle, she saw something that made her heart stop.

Chapter 18
Conjuring

conjuring (v) making something appear unexpectedly, as if out of nowhere; (n) the performance of magic tricks

Evan was good at stage patter, but he couldn't keep talking like this forever. He had already walked three times around the basket, pointing out that it was truly empty and that Jessie had disappeared into thin air. Then he had turned the basket upright again and refastened the lid. Then he had lifted the basket off the ground, carefully holding the false bottom in place, to show that there was nothing *under* the basket.

"My assistant is gone! Disappeared! Vanished! Who knows if we will ever see her again?" The audience was completely silent, staring in wonder at the stage. Evan felt as though he had cast a spell over them. But it was a spell that wouldn't last forever. Where *was* Jessie? Why didn't she appear at the back of the audience as they had planned?

Maybe she was stuck under the porch? Could she have hurt herself when she fell through the hole? Maybe she'd gotten so scared in the basket that she'd fainted after escaping. Evan scanned the back of the audience, trying to see if there was any movement in the woods. She should have appeared by now. Something must have gone horribly wrong.

He was just about to announce that the show was over, pull the curtains closed, and go through the hole in search of Jessie, when he saw her sneaking through the trees behind the audience. What a relief! She was probably just being her usual klutzy self, taking twice as long to crawl out from under the porch as anyone else. That was Jessie!

"Yes, she's gone!" he called out to the audience. "Gone! But I have the power to bring her back! With a wave of my magic wand—one, two, three!"—Evan swished his wand in giant circles, as if he were scooping up the air and gathering it into a powerful cyclone—"I will make her reappear! As you can see!" As Evan pointed his wand to the back of the audience, everyone in the backyard turned. When they saw Jessie standing there, they burst into wild applause.

"And look what I can make reappear!" yelled Jessie over the loud applause as she walked to the stage. "Professor Hoffmann!" She raised both hands over her head so that everyone could see the small white rabbit she held.

Evan shouted, "Woohoo! That's all, folks!" and jumped down off the stage. He rushed up to Jessie and put both his hands on Professor Hoffmann, just to be sure he was real. He'd learned enough about smoke and mirrors to know that you couldn't always trust your eyes, but touching the rabbit's soft fur and feeling his familiar twitch convinced him that the rabbit was back from the dead. "He was in the woods?" asked Evan.

"No!" whispered Jessie. "He was under the porch. There's a tiny hole in the foundation. Tiny!" She held up her hand and made a circle about the size of a half-dollar. "He must have squeezed through it! And he's been hiding under the porch ever since."

"Wow! *He's* the escape artist! We should call him Houdini," said Evan.

"Nope. He's Professor Hoffmann, and he's never going anywhere again." Jessie lifted the rabbit to her face and laid her cheek against his soft fur. She loved Professor Hoffmann. He had survived a Category 1 hurricane, too, just like them.

"Take a bow!" said Megan. So Evan and Jessie jumped back up onstage and bowed over and over again as the audience applauded and whistled and shouted "Bravo!" Evan had the feeling that Jessie would stay up there all day, but he could tell that Professor Hoffmann was getting jumpy, so he called out, "Show's over!" and people started trailing away. Jessie put Professor Hoffmann safely in his rabbit box with a whole lettuce leaf. Evan knew that if the rabbit pooped, he'd be the one who had to clean it, but that was okay. Jessie had done such a great job with the Amazing Disappearing Trick that he didn't mind taking care of doody duty.

They were hauling a large branch over to the side yard when Evan saw something that made him forget everything else.

"Mom!" he shouted, dropping the branch and running full speed at his mother. By the time he wrapped his arms around her and breathed in her familiar smell (green tea shampoo and powdered laundry detergent), Jessie was pulling on their mother's arm. Evan wasn't sure why, but he suddenly started crying, and then his mother started crying, too!

"We got a rabbit!" announced Jessie.

"What?" asked their mother, disentangling herself from Evan's full-body hug. Evan glared at Jessie. He didn't think that was the best beginning to their mom's return.

"His name is Professor Hoffmann. He was supposed to be part of our magic show. That's why Dad got him. But then he couldn't be in the show because we thought he had died because . . . because . . . he . . ." Jessie's voice stumbled and faltered and then simply collapsed into silence.

"A rabbit? Huh." Their mother shook her head, and Evan could see a trace of annoyance on her face. "Let me talk to your dad about that." She started to walk around the side of the house and into the backyard, but she stopped dead when she saw the Climbing Tree.

"Oh, my God!" she said.

Jessie started to jump up and down. "It landed on my bed! Right on my bed! Evan saved my life because he told me to sleep in your bed. When we woke up, there was a sound like a cannon going off! *Kapow!*"

"Why didn't Dad call me? When did this happen?" Then Evan saw that their mother was staring at the porch. The railing was missing, but not in jagged pieces. It was cleanly removed. "Evan, did the storm take off the porch railing?"

"No . . ." said Evan. "Dad took it down because he said it wasn't safe. He already called someone to repair it, but I don't remember the name . . ."

"He took it down?" said their mother, repeating the words as if they couldn't possibly be right. "He took down *my* porch railing? Where *is* your father?" As she talked, she climbed onto the porch and headed for the kitchen door.

"Don't step there!" Evan shouted as his mother was about to cross the rug.

"My rug!" said their mother. "Evan! Jessie! You know you're not allowed to take anything from my office." She bent over and picked up the wet rug, revealing the hole underneath.

No one said a word. Their mother looked at the hole, and now Evan could see that she was *furious.* Was she mad at him? He had wanted her to come home, but not so she would be mad at him. Suddenly he felt so tired, as if he'd been holding up the whole house for two days. He had tried to keep everything together—but the house was in ruins. And his mom hadn't even seen the leaks in the ceilings or the flooded basement. How angry was she going to get?

"I need to talk with Dad," she said, her voice strangely quiet. "Where is he?"

Evan and Jessie just stared at her. Evan was

petrified that Jessie was going to say something and just as scared that she wouldn't say anything and leave it all up to him to explain.

Their mother looked at them, one, then the other, then back again. "Where is he?" she repeated, but this time her voice was so taut that Evan knew she was even more scared than they were.

"He left," said Jessie.

"What do you mean?" asked their mother, her voice as small as a pinprick.

"He just left," said Evan. It was awful to say out loud. What kind of father leaves his kids? "He went back to the war."

Their mother took a step back, as if she'd been hit. Evan worried that she would retreat to the edge of the porch and maybe fall off. There was no railing to protect her.

"When did he leave?" she asked slowly, as if these words were foreign and she wasn't quite sure of their pronunciation.

Jessie started to whine. "Mommy . . ."

Evan took three steps toward his mom. If she was going to fall, he wanted to be close enough to grab her and hold on. "He left Saturday morning, before the storm. He needed to catch a flight out. That's why you couldn't reach his cell phone. He was flying."

"You've been *alone?*" Their mother started to cry. "You've been alone for *two days?* You were alone during the storm? When the tree fell?"

Tears fell down her cheeks, a slow, steady drip that made Evan think of the leaking ceiling during the storm.

"Come here," said their mother, her voice a little stronger. "Come here." They ran up to her, careful to avoid the jagged hole in the porch floor, and even Jessie let herself be held by the arm. "I'm so sorry. I'm so, so sorry. I never should have left you. I don't know what I was thinking."

This made Evan mad. It wasn't his mom's fault. Why did she have to feel bad just for doing her job? "No, you *should* have gone," he said. "You had to go. We know that. It's not your fault. You didn't do anything wrong."

"And besides," said Jessie. "We did great! We did everything right. Evan and me. We patched up the hole in the wall, and we didn't open the refrigerator, and we emptied the buckets, and we kept the rain off the floor, and we did the magic show perfectly, and we even found Professor Hoffmann. Well, *I* found Professor Hoffmann. That was just me."

Evan shook his head. Jessie always liked to get extra credit. But she made their mom laugh, so inside his head Evan said, *Good job, Jess!*

And then he thought that she was right: They *did* do a good job. With all the worry and chaos and destruction, he'd lost sight of that accomplishment.

"But, Mom?" asked Jessie in her matter-of-fact voice. "Why does Dad always leave us?"

Their mom sat down on the porch, as if her legs couldn't hold her weight any longer. Evan and Jessie sat down right next to her, one on each side. Evan held his breath, waiting to hear what she would say. He had been waiting a long time to hear the answer to this question.

"Your dad loves you very much, and he's a good man. He's smart and generous and fun—and tough." Mrs. Treski looked beyond the porch and into the woods, as if the words she was searching for were hidden among the trees. "But some people—some very good people—just aren't meant to be parents. They're not so good at it. That doesn't make them bad, and you can still love them. But it's something you need to know and understand. So you can protect yourselves. Just like you did during the storm. You took good care of yourselves and each other. You're the best kids in the whole world, and I'm the luckiest mom on the planet."

Evan let his mother's words sink in. Then he smiled for what felt like the first time all week. He'd been hoping that things were going to be different this time. But they weren't. His dad was—Dad. The sooner he accepted that, the better off he would be. Still, he didn't want to hate his father. His dad was a part of him, and hating him was like hating a part of himself.

Jessie shook her head solemnly. "I wouldn't say you're the luckiest mom on the planet. Not until you look inside the house."

Her mom groaned. "How bad is it? Wait, don't tell me. Let's just go look."

Jessie and their mother went inside, but Evan

stayed in the yard. He wandered over to the Climbing Tree and rested his hand on its trunk. Then, he bowed his head until his forehead was touching the rough, damp bark and whispered, "Goodbye."

*   *   *

Later that afternoon, after Mrs. Treski had seen all the damage and then double-checked their insurance policy to make sure that they really were covered for hurricanes and flooding, Evan and Jessie had a meeting in Evan's room. When they went downstairs, they found their mother sitting at the kitchen table trying to figure out how to fix the porch. Insurance wasn't going to pay for that. She had a notepad full of scribbled numbers.

"How much will it cost?" asked Jessie. She was standing next to her mother with both hands behind her back. Her stomach felt excited but in a good way.

"A lot," said Mrs. Treski grimly.

"But how much? Exactly?"

Mrs. Treski shook her head. "I don't know. Pete said he'd drive down and take a look at it."

"Pete!" shouted Evan. It had been five months since he'd seen Pete. "We can do it! Me and Pete together! You won't have to hire anyone." A huge grin broke out on Evan's face.

"It's still going to cost a lot . . ."

"But how much?" asked Jessie, looking at Evan. He looked back at her, and his grin grew even wider.

"I don't know . . ."

"More than one hundred and twenty-seven dollars?"

Mrs. Treski looked at her, raising one eyebrow. "Why do you ask that?"

Jessie pulled both hands from behind her back and held them out for her mother to see. They were filled with dollar bills.

"We made one hundred and twenty-seven dollars at the magic show today, and we want you to have it . . . all." That last word was hard for Jessie. It had been Evan's idea to give the magic show money to their mother, but Jessie had agreed. Still, it was a struggle for her to give up every last penny.

Mrs. Treski smiled. "This is really nice of you, but . . ."

"We *think* there should have been one hundred and twenty-*eight* dollars, since the tickets were two dollars apiece, which means the total *shouldn't* be an odd number, but maybe someone paid just one dollar instead." Jessie scowled. She didn't like it when there were math errors. Or when someone didn't follow the rules and pay the right price. "Probably Scott Spencer. I bet . . ." She crossed her arms. "Well. We don't have any evidence, so I guess we don't know. For *sure.*"

"Anyway," said Evan, "we want you to have the money. We know it's not enough, but it's something, right?"

"Are you kidding? It's huge," said Mrs. Treski. "But I don't want to take your money. You worked so hard."

"But we're Treskis, and Treskis—" Jessie stopped. Somehow she couldn't quite bring herself to say what her dad always said. It didn't feel right. Instead she said, "Treskis stick together."

"Yeah," said Evan. "Like you always say. Family comes first."

"Thank you both," said Mrs. Treski. She gave

Evan a big hug and put her hand on Jessie's head, then took the money and put it in an envelope with her pages of calculations. "This makes a big difference," she said before going upstairs.

That made Jessie feel better, but it was still hard to lose all that money. She wondered if she would ever be able to open her own bank account.

She turned to look at Evan, who had pulled a quarter from his pocket and was making it dance across his knuckles. The flashing coin made Jessie think of something.

"Hey, Evan," she said. "*I've* got an idea."

Evan looked at his sister.

Jessie planted her feet and put her hands on her hips. "It's hot outside, right?"

"Yeah."

"So we could have . . ."

Evan flipped the quarter into the air and Jessie caught it as it fell.

". . . a lemonade stand!" they both shouted.

How to Perform:
The Mixed-Up Kings

1. You must perform this trick seated behind a table or a desk so that no one can see your lap.

2. Before you begin the trick, make sure you have four cards in your lap that no one can see. It doesn't matter what these cards are as long as they're not kings.

3. Fan out the cards in the deck to show your audience that there's nothing special about the deck. Say, "This is a story of four kings who were brothers." Search through the deck

and remove the four kings. You are now holding four kings in your right hand and the rest of the deck in your left hand.

4. Then say, "I'm going to put the kings in my lap so I know where they are." As you lower the king cards, drop both hands behind the table and do the following: place the four king cards at the bottom of the deck *facing in the opposite direction* of all the other cards.

5. Saying, "Once again, notice that there's nothing unusual about this deck of cards," hold the deck up and fan the cards out in your hand so that the audience sees the backs of the cards, but *do not reveal* that the four kings are facing in the opposite direction at the bottom of the deck.

The four king cards are hidden at the bottom of the deck, face-up!

6. Say, "Now the kings are going to travel to the four corners of the earth. The first king will go to the North." Pick up one of the cards from your lap and hold it up for the audience *so that they see the back of the card*. They will assume it's a king card, but it's actually not. Place the card somewhere in the deck.

7. Say, "The second king will go to the South." Pick up one of the cards from your lap and hold it up. Place the card somewhere in the deck.

8. Say, "The third king will go to the East." Pick up one of the cards from your lap and hold it up. Place the card somewhere in the deck.

9. Say, "And the fourth king will go to the West." Pick up the last card from your lap and place it somewhere in the deck.

10. Say, "But the kings' troubles are just beginning. An evil sorcerer has decided to create chaos by mixing Up with Down, In with Out, Right with Wrong! Watch as I shuffle the cards with half the deck face-up and half the deck face-down."

11. Cut the cards so that you are holding the top half of the deck in your right hand and the bottom half of the deck (with the four king cards hidden at the bottom) in your left hand. At the same time, as if preparing to shuffle, flip both halves of the decks over. Now the kings are on the top of the cards in your left hand. It will appear that you are about to shuffle half the deck face-down and half the deck face-up—but you are really shuffling all the cards face-up except for the four king cards.

The four king cards are on the top of this pille!

12. Shuffle the cards again and again, explaining how confused and lost the kings will be.

13. Say, "How will the kings ever find their way home? Can you help them?"

14. Invite the audience to say the magic spell: "Kings: Come home, come home, you will no longer roam." Then spread out the cards *face-up* on the table and extract the only four face-down cards: they will be the four king cards.

251

ACKNOWLEDGMENTS

So many people helped put the magic in this book: thanks to my editor, Ann Rider; my agent, Tracey Adams; and the whole team at Houghton Mifflin Harcourt who've been on this journey from the first: Cara Llewellyn, Christine Krones, Ann-Marie Pucillo, Mary Huot, Karen Walsh, and Lisa DiSarro. It's a pleasure to work alongside people who have such a deep and abiding commitment to bringing good books to young readers.

I'd like to thank my handwriting guys: Ryle Sammut, who provided Evan's handwriting, and my brother, Tom Davies, who provided the perfectly careless handwriting for Mr. Treski.

I am indebted to a trio of top-notch meteorologists who explained the intricacies of early-season hurricanes to me: Harvey Leonard, chief meteorologist, and Mike Wankum, meteorologist, of WCVB-TV in Boston; and Dan Skeldon, chief meteorologist of NBC40 in New Jersey.

Also, thanks to the amazing magical team of Penn & Teller, who patiently demonstrated the Seven Basic Principles of Magic on their YouTube video. I watched it twenty times and still couldn't catch the ditch. The Mixed-Up Kings card trick is inspired by a card trick of the same name in Joshua Jay's excellent book, *Magic: The Complete Course*. And to the magician who was one of the first to lift the curtain for us mere mortals and explain how it's all done: Professor Hoffman, I offer my thanks and admiration.

My writers group is never outside my circle of gratitude. I'd like to thank Carol Peacock, Sarah Lamstein, Tracey Fern, and Mary Atkinson. They're always *there*.

I began this book with a thank-you to my father, and I'd like to end with one to my whole family of origin: my mother, Ann Davies; my sisters, Leslie and Kim Davies; and, again, my brother, Tom. Also, heartfelt thanks and endless amounts of love to my own three children, who are more miraculous to me than any magic trick: Mae, Henry, and Sam. *Now you see 'em, now you don't.*

THE REAL PROFESSOR HOFFMANN

Professor Hoffmann was a real person, but his actual name was Angelo John Lewis. Born in London on July 23, 1839, Lewis learned his first magic from his French teacher, who taught him tricks as a reward for doing good schoolwork.

But Lewis had no thoughts of being a professional magician. At that time, magicians were an odd group. They wore pointy hats and dressed in long robes with enormous sleeves that were covered with strange, mystical symbols. Many of them had long, flowing beards. In fact, they looked a lot like Dumbledore, the character in the Harry Potter books who is styled after the ancient mythical wizard Merlin of King Arthur's court.

So Lewis went on to study at Oxford (a very prestigious university in England) and became a lawyer—a much more respectable profession than being a magician.

But even as he practiced law, he continued to be interested in magic. He collected books on magic and magical apparatuses that helped magicians perform tricks. He even put on a few amateur shows of his own.

In 1874, he sent a letter to the publishers of *Boy's Magazine* and asked them if they'd like to publish some of his articles on magic. They agreed to publish a whole series of articles and then publish those articles as a book after they appeared in the magazine. The book was titled *Modern Magic,* and it was published in 1876. The publishers didn't pay Lewis much money for his writing. In fact, they paid more than three times as much for the illustrations!

But why didn't Lewis use his own name? At the time, he was still a practicing lawyer, and he didn't want his colleagues to think that he was a trickster. "I did not think that being known to dabble in magic would increase my professional prestige," he said. So he created the persona of Professor Hoffmann, and that is how he is known to this day.

His book has been described as "a bombshell among conjurers at the time" because it championed the "new style" of magic performed by Jean Eugene Robert-Houdin. Robert-Houdin was a French magician who gave up the flowing robes and pointy hats of earlier times and dressed like an "ordinary gentleman," which in the late 1800s meant a necktie, a formal dress coat with tails, and a top hat. Like Robert-Houdin, Lewis encouraged magicians to give up the trappings of the old ways and perform magic as an ordinary person doing extraordinary things.

Also, *Modern Magic* was the first book in English that described how tricks were done using simple, clear, step-by-step language. Lewis wrote like a lawyer: logically and with an eye for details. Many people had been waiting for just such a book because it taught them *how* to perform magic tricks.

Not surprisingly, *Modern Magic* was an instant success. The first printing of 2,000 copies sold out in just seven weeks. More than a century later, the book is still in print and is considered a classic on the art of conjuring. Harry Houdini (birth name Eric Weisz, who chose his new name to sound like Robert-Houdin's) called Lewis "The Brightest Star in the Firmament of Magical Literature."

Lewis wrote dozens of books and articles on magic and even

wrote a novel for young children that had magic as a theme. He never performed magic professionally, but every once in a while he would put on a show and give all the proceeds to charity. In 1903, Lewis retired to the quiet seaside town of Hastings, and in 1919, at the age of eighty, he died.

On the title page of the American edition of *Modern Magic* are the Latin words *Populus vult decipi: decipiatur*. This phrase means "People want to be deceived." At its root, that's how magic works. People want to be tricked, and magicians oblige. Over the years, Professor Hoffmann has brought the world of happy deception to millions of readers.

The other
Professor Hoffmann!

Book 1: The Lemonade War

Evan Treski is people-smart. He is good at talking with people, even grownups. His younger sister, Jessie, on the other hand, is math-smart—but not especially good at understanding people. She knows that feelings are her weakest subject. So when their lemonade war begins, there really is no telling who will win—and even more important, if their fight will ever end.

Here is a clever blend of humor and math fun. As it captures the one-of-a-kind bond between brother and sister, this poignant novel subtly explores how arguments can escalate beyond anyone's intent.

A Booklinks Lasting Choice
A New York Public Library 100 Titles for Reading and Sharing Selection

"A funny, fresh, and plausible novel with likable characters."
—*School Library Journal*

"Lemonade stands, entrepreneurial schemes, and dirty tricks find their way into the competition. . . . Davies does a good job of showing the siblings' strengths, flaws, and points of view in this engaging chapter book."
—*Booklist*

"Entertaining. . . . Good reading for young capitalists."
—*USA Today*

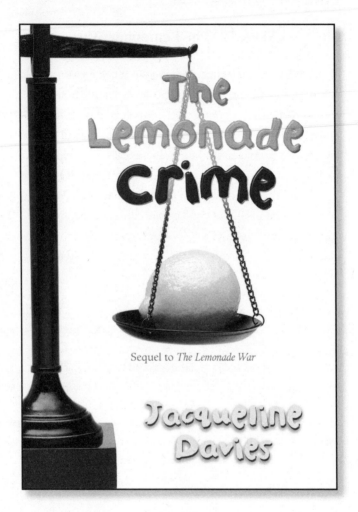

The
Lemonade
Crime

Sequel to *The Lemonade War*

Jacqueline
Davies

Book 2 : The Lemonade Crime

In the much-anticipated sequel to bestseller *The Lemonade War,* brother and sister duo Evan and Jessie turn the playground into a full-blown courtroom and attempt to take the law into their own hands. This engaging chapter book entertains and explores the issue of fairness.

★ "The realistic depiction of the children's emotions and ways of expressing them will resonate with readers. Great for discussion, this involving and at times riveting chapter book has something to say and a deceptively simple way of saying it."
—*Booklist,* starred review

"Short chapters, realistic dialogue and social dynamics, humor, and suspense will keep even reluctant readers turning pages to the satisfying conclusion. *The Lemonade Crime* is certainly a first purchase for collections that have *The Lemonade War.* But it can stand alone and would make a lovely read-aloud, especially in tween classrooms, where it's all about justice and fairness."
—*School Library Journal*

The Lemonade War Series

The Bell Bandit

Jacqueline Davies

Book 3: The Bell Bandit

Unforgettable brother-sister duo Evan and Jessie are back in the third installment of the best-selling Lemonade War series. Can they solve the mystery of who stole the New Year's Bell?

A Junior Library Guild Selection
Bank Street Books Best Children's Book of the Year 2013

"With this highly readable and yet emotionally powerful novel, Davies is proving herself one of the best writers for the middle grades around."
—*Books for Kids*

Book 4: The Candy Smash

Poignant and funny, this fourth book in the best-selling Lemonade War series is a Valentine mystery full of sweet (and sour) surprises.

Winter 2012-13 Kids' Indie Next List

"Another rewarding chapter book from the Lemonade War series."
—*Booklist*

"A terrific tie-in to Valentine's Day, but a good anytime school story for boys and girls alike."
—*Read Kiddo Read*

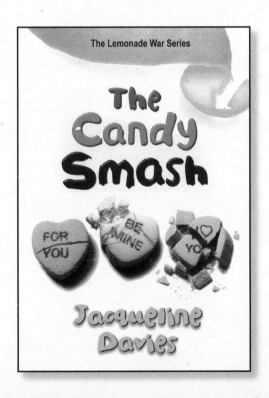